MW00877814

EDEN LOST

Eden Rising Post-Apocalyptic Series
Book Two

Andrew Cunningham

Copyright © 2014 Andrew Cunningham

All rights reserved.

ISBN-13: 978-1499129274
ISBN-10: 1499129270

Books by Andrew Cunningham

Thrillers
Wisdom Spring
Deadly Shore

Yestertime Time Travel Series
Yestertime
The Yestertime Effect
The Yestertime Warning

"Lies" Mystery Series
All Lies
Fatal Lies
Vegas Lies
Secrets & Lies
Blood Lies
Buried Lies

Eden Rising Series
Eden Rising
Eden Lost
Eden's Legacy
Eden's Survival

Children's Mysteries (as A.R Cunningham)
The Arthur MacArthur Mysteries: The Complete Series

Thank you to everyone who helped in some way in the creation of this book: Charlotte and Alma for your constant support, your reading of the manuscript, and suggestions to make it better; Chris and Ashlee for correcting my misguided Marine-speak, getting the weapons to shoot correctly, and a few other items. Any errors are my own (hey, sometimes I just don't pay attention); to Ms. Gager, my 8th-grade English teacher at Elvira Castro Junior High School, in San Jose, CA, who gave me an A- on my short story, with the words "Good dialogue." Whether it was true, or you just knew how important it was to me (considering I was bugging you every day) and were being supportive, it had a major impact on my decision to someday become a writer. And lastly, thank you to Camden, who continues to show me just how capable, intuitive, and intelligent a six-year-old can be. You were the inspiration for Katie's self-sufficiency.

To Charlotte … forever

Prologue

Seven years ago the world died.

I often think about who we were before the catastrophe. I was seventeen, and Lila was a year younger. In so many ways we were both behind others our age in maturity. But then I wonder about that. Were we really? Because somehow we ended up alive when so many other "survivors" of the event couldn't make it.

We learned self-preservation in a hurry. We saw some of the worst of humanity and some of the best. Sadly, I think the worst overshadowed the best. But maybe that was what we needed to experience in order to gain the skills and the strength to keep going.

Our story of overcoming adversity became a rallying cry for some. "The Legend of Ben and Lila" was a source of hope for so many. We became folk heroes up and down the east coast. And then we disappeared. We never wanted the folk hero label. It was thrust upon us by others—the scared, the needy, and those without hope. I often wonder how many of those people made it beyond the first year.

It was a massive electro-magnetic pulse from a nuclear weapon originating from our own country—from our own (now late) president—that was the cause. So powerful, it wreaked havoc with the human electrical system, killing anyone who wasn't lucky enough to be far enough underground—or in an industrial freezer, as Lila and I were. All electricity died along with the humans. We have to assume it was a world-wide event, because we've never seen a plane, or any indications that other countries fared better than us.

So Lila and I faded into the background. Our journey away from the death and destruction toward a peaceful life was a hard one. We often had to bring ourselves down to match the lowest level of human consciousness in order to survive. But somehow we did, and we found what we were searching for—a remote cabin on the shores of a beautiful lake in the Great Smoky Mountains. Away from humanity—what was left of it—we could live our life in peace. That's all we wanted.

In the months following the great catastrophe, we developed the skills to live off the land, to defend ourselves, and to defend others when necessary. Often it was skill, and sometimes we were just lucky.

But our luck couldn't hold out forever....

Chapter 1

Something was wrong.

It was the animals. There was too much activity. They were spooked.

Ben leaned his crossbow against a tree and looked down at his daughter. Mimicking her father, Katie set her crossbow next to his. Katie was using Ben's old pistol crossbow, a miniature version of the full-sized model Ben now used. It was still too big for her, and Ben carried it for her most of the time, but she could use it. At six, she had become amazingly accurate with it.

Katie looked up at the sky through a break in the foliage.

"Look at the birds, Daddy."

"I see them kiddo." Flocks of them streaked across the sky. Too many. He pointed up the trail. "See the bears?" A mother and a cub. Normally he would try to stay hidden and not tempt fate by letting the mother see them. Not this time. The bears were ignoring them. They had other concerns at the moment. Animals possessed a great awareness of the earth. Could it be that another earthquake was coming?

The ground hadn't shaken since the devastating

earthquake right after Katie was born. That one changed the landscape forever. No more earthquakes, but the weather was still violent on a regular basis. Ben wasn't sure that would ever change. The cataclysmic event of seven years earlier—the one that had stripped the world of so much of its population—had also done something to the climate. An accelerated climate change was the opinion of their friend Nick, who had been working as a meteorologist at the time of the event and had warned them of the coming quake when they first met on the trail.

Whatever the explanation, the violent storms had become a normal part of their life. In fact, Ben and Katie had had to seek shelter just an hour earlier when a fierce storm quickly passed through.

Three deer burst out of the forest and crossed the trail right in front of them.

"Something's making the animals scared, Daddy."

Ben was constantly amazed by his daughter's awareness at her young age. But he knew that it came from spending her whole life surrounded by nature. She knew nothing of the distractions he had grown up with—TV, video games, movies … noise in general. She only knew peace. She lived as one with the animals, the trees, and the lake. She sensed weather patterns and lunar activity. Nobody taught her these things.

"I smell smoke."

Ben smelled it too. His heart sank. A fire. A forest fire. With the violent weather, it was a constant fear they had had to live with. Up until now, they had been spared.

"We need to get back to the house … quickly!"

Ben picked up the two crossbows. He didn't have to worry

about Katie. She was fast and was already way ahead of him. She knew her way in the forest. He hoped Lila could smell the smoke back at the cabin. If so, she'd start the preparation, carrying the essentials down to the beach. If not, they'd be there in twenty minutes. He could only hope that the fire wasn't blowing their way.

As he ran along the narrow trail, branches whipping his face, he thought of everything that needed to be done. They had made a checklist of items—in order of importance—that they needed to get down to the beach in case of a fire. But that was only the first step. The beach was close to the tree line and not totally safe from the heat the fire would generate. Step two was to load the boats. He and Lila had accumulated a few boats over the years, and the goal was to fill them with the important items and row the boats, all connected by rope, out to the center of the lake. If they couldn't get everything into the boats, at least their things left on the beach had a chance of survival. This would have been a good time to have an outboard motor, but Ben hadn't found any gas in well over a year.

Ben arrived to find Lila transporting armloads to the beach. She had seen the black smoke in the distance and had immediately gone to work. Katie was already there, helping to carry some of the smaller items out, and Ralph, her dog and best friend, was running back and forth, barking at the smoke.

"I saw the smoke and prayed that you and Katie did too," said Lila.

Ben detected the fear in her voice.

"Katie knew before me," answered Ben. "She sensed it."

They worked tirelessly, carrying weapons and ammunition, camping gear, emergency food, the few personal items they had accumulated, and other things on their list down to the beach. Ben also grabbed the antique meat grinder.

One of their most joyous finds a few years earlier had been a crank meat grinder. They missed burgers, and the grinder allowed them to turn whatever meat they had—venison, bear, and even pork and beef from the occasional pig and cow they ran across—into burgers. One of the few reminders of their old life.

The fire was getting steadily closer, the pungent smell of smoke becoming stronger. Ben started to load the boats while Lila looked for any items that might not have made the list. They had four boats large enough to carry their possessions. They pushed the kayaks and canoes out into the lake. They wouldn't float far, but it might be enough keep them from being destroyed.

Ben could feel the heat and see the flames above the treetops. The boats wouldn't fit everything, so he dug a hole in the sand, threw the remaining items in, and covered them with the sand.

"We need to go."

Lila had roped the four boats in a line. They pushed the first one out.

"Take Katie," said Lila, "and start rowing. I'll push the others out, then swim to you." She lifted Katie into the first boat with Ben and gave her a kiss. Up until then, Katie hadn't shown any signs of fear, but now she could see the flames and hear the roar of the fire.

"It's okay, kiddo," Ben assured her. "We'll be safe and mom will be here in a minute."

Ralph jumped into the second boat where there was a little

more room for him.

Ben started rowing. It was hard work with the other three boats trailing behind. Over the years, though, he had developed a strong upper body. Besides, they didn't have to go too far out onto the lake; just enough to escape the heat.

Lila caught up to them and lifted herself into the boat. She stepped over the pile of belongings and sat on the bench next to Katie, in front of Ben, who was still rowing. Finally, they were far enough out and Ben retracted the oars and moved onto the bench next to his family and put his arm around the two of them.

The fire was massive and seemed to be on all sides of the lake.

"What about the animals?" asked Katie in a small voice.

"I'm sure they made it out okay," said Lila, glancing at Ben, and knowing it was a lie.

They sat in silence as they watched the flames come closer to, and finally consume their garden—which was at the end of its summer production. Next came the smokehouse, the outhouse, and finally their home of the past six years. It was their Eden, their refuge from all the negativity they had encountered after the event. It was the only home Katie had known. It was where Ben and Lila had reveled in their new found love for each other. There would be no rebuilding it. Even if they could rebuild, it would be years before the post-fire new growth of the forest would support them.

No, they were going to have to leave their paradise.

Ben looked over at Lila.

A single tear rolled down her cheek.

Chapter 2

The last three years hadn't been kind to Lila. Somehow, I was able to skate through our years on the shores of Fontana Lake without any serious injury or sickness. Lila made it through the first three years unscathed, but the last three had been disastrous.

It began with the miscarriages—two of them. We had decided Katie needed a sibling and were so excited when Lila got pregnant. But then she lost the baby. It devastated us both, but Lila took it particularly hard. When she lost the second one we stopped trying—I wasn't sure we ever would again.

Then came the broken ankle. She stepped in a hole that was camouflaged by grass. It was a bad break. I was twenty feet from her and heard the crack. We had books that instructed us on how to set it, but I wasn't a doctor. There was only so much I could do. I set it as best I could, and eventually Lila healed, but she was left with an ever-so-slight limp—not really noticeable unless she was tired or stressed. But I could see it, and I knew that there was a residual pain that she had to live with on a constant basis, but that she wouldn't admit to.

But breaking her ankle paled in comparison to her accident a few months later. It was a freak occurrence. We were in the woods hunting mushrooms. Lila had just picked one from under a tree and was standing up when a deer crashed through the branches and ran off. Maybe it was escaping a predator, or maybe we startled it. All I know is that Lila's scream will forever be imprinted in my memory. We never knew if it was the deer's antler that clipped her or if one of the branches speared her and sprang back. She clutched her eye and I knew it was bad. The pain was unbearable, and there was blood streaming down her face. We did everything we could, but in the end, the eye was destroyed. Her right eye—her shooting eye.

In our new life, our senses were everything. They were a vital part of our survival. To have her senses depleted like that was a terrible blow to Lila.

And now the fire....

Ben looked over at Lila, sitting in the boat, watching their cabin burn. She fiddled with her eye-patch, a habit she had picked up. A three-quarter inch scar peeked out from the bottom of the patch. A thin line, it was shaped like a backward comma and almost looked like a teardrop. Seeing that brought Ben back to the days and months following the loss of her eye.

*****

Lila had grown into quite a beautiful woman. But losing her eye made her feel like damaged goods. She retreated into herself, not talking for long periods of time. Sex became non-existent between them, as she felt she had lost any desirability. Nothing Ben said could convince her otherwise.

He made a special trip into one of the surrounding towns to find a black eye-patch—to complement her long raven-colored hair—but it didn't seem to change her opinion of herself or her outlook.

Katie could see the difference in her mood, and Ben tried to use that as a way to bring her back. But it didn't work. Lila was mired in a deep depression and didn't show any signs of coming out of it. She went about her life without saying much. Ben took over many of the duties of raising Katie. Katie seemed to understand—or maybe she was just too young to know what was happening.

This went on for over four months. Ben tried his best not to get frustrated with her, but seeing her lost in her own world was hard for him and he found himself snapping at her on an increasingly frequent basis.

And then things changed. Ben wasn't sure how or why they changed, but he wasn't about to question it. Maybe she just got tired of being depressed, and the old Lila was trying to break through. One night Lila rolled over in bed and touched him—tentatively, as if trying to gauge his response. He gently touched her back, and then held her hand. They fell asleep that way. Each night over the next week he'd feel her getting closer and more trusting, until finally she let him embrace her fully. That was the night she cried—silently at first, then progressing into a long, mournful wail. It lasted forever.

They made love the next night for the first time in months, and the healing began. Over the next few weeks, Lila started to come out of her shell—slowly at first, and then a little more each day. She began to re-establish her bond with both Ben and Katie. Katie was thrilled to have her mother back and Ben could see the connection between them returning.

That was a year ago. Lila was almost back to being the strong woman who had supported and loved him for so long. She had finally accepted her impairment, and was even making the most of the eye patch. She styled her hair so that black wisps floated over the patch, giving her a mysterious look. To Ben, she was more beautiful than ever. She never talked much about her depressed period, but that was okay with Ben. It was the past. All he cared about was that he finally had Lila back.

But now, yet another disaster. How was she going to react?

*****

They sat in the boat for hours. Ben would occasionally row them out further when they started to drift too close to shore. Little was said. They were all trying to deal with the loss in their own way.

Night came, but still they remained on the water. The flames had long since extinguished themselves with little left to burn, but the heat was still uncomfortable and there were small pockets of fire in the stumps. Lila and Katie had fallen asleep in each other's arms in the bottom of the boat, using the pile of belongings for support. Ben reached over and covered his family with a blanket. And then he allowed himself a cry.

It was a quiet moment of grief—he didn't want Lila or Katie to hear him. He cried for the loss of their home, the loss of the forest and its abundant life, and for the unknown of what lay ahead for them.

With the morning light, Ben rowed back to shore. Lila and Katie were awake, surveying the devastation around them.

"It looks so different," was Katie's observation. "Will we have to leave?" Although Katie hadn't yet cried over the loss of her home, Ben could tell that the tears were always on the verge of erupting. She was trying to be brave and grown-up.

"We will, honey," answered Lila.

"Where will we go?"

Lila looked at Ben. He had no answers.

"We'll find an awesome place to live," Ben said. "Something different, but just as good."

That sounded lame, he thought.

They set up a tent on the beach and took stock of their belongings. If they left Fontana Lake, most of what they saved from the cabin would have to remain behind.

"You know," said Ben, looking out across the lake. "Not all of the forest was destroyed. There's a whole section untouched. We could always move over there and look for another cabin."

Lila just shook her head.

Katie was down the beach exploring with Ralph. A mix of many breeds, predominantly Lab, Ralph was almost as tall as Katie.

"We need to find someplace with people," Lila said quietly.

"But you've always loved the fact that we weren't around people," answered Ben.

Lila looked at Ben with a misty eye. "Katie needs other children in her life and it doesn't look like I'll be able to provide that for her. It's great that she is so in tune with nature, but she needs more. We can't live here anymore."

"Where do you want to go? We have no idea where we'll find other children."

"Back when we were coming here, some people were going further south—to Florida. Maybe there? Or maybe to Washington. Your friend, President Jeffries, was trying to rebuild."

Lila didn't want to do either of those things. Ben could tell. She was really struggling. But she had a point. Maybe it was time for Katie to be with other children. Were they depriving her somehow? If they were still living alone in the woods when Katie hit her teenage years, would it be unfair to her to not be able to experience love. Would it be too late at that point? She needed to start interacting with others before then.

It wasn't that he was afraid to venture out. After all, he and Lila had shared an amazing adventure together getting there. But he had gotten used to his home by the lake, and things were different now. They had Katie. They couldn't take the chances they once took.

And were they prepared? Ben hadn't had to fire his guns in almost two years. They didn't like the noise in their little paradise. All of their hunting had been with the crossbow. Could they defend themselves the way they once did? But Lila had a point.

"You're right," Ben finally admitted. "I hadn't really thought about Katie as a teenager and how this life might actually stunt her in some ways."

"It's been in the back of my mind for a while," said Lila, "but I couldn't bear the thought of leaving here. The decision was made for us. We always thought we'd eventually do some more traveling. I guess that time has come."

Ben's fears about how Lila would respond to the fire had been put to rest. She was definitely the Lila of old—clear-thinking and optimistic.

"We're going to have to walk, at least until we find some gas—and a car that will run." He reflected for a moment, then shook his head. "Not that a car would be of any use."

The electro-magnetic pulse—EMP—had affected anything that had a circuit board, and most electrical systems in general, so they had found early on that the only vehicles that worked were old, pre-computer cars. Some of the older outboard engines were usable, and were a great help on the lake. But the available gas eventually ran out. Gas pumps didn't work, and Ben lacked the knowledge to access the gas stored in the tanks below the ground. For a long time, he had siphoned gas from other cars, but even that was no longer viable. Many of the cars had rusted, their tanks leaking out all the gas, and in most of those that were still intact, the gas had fouled—full of dirt, rust, or water. Ben had finally given up looking. They had everything they needed by the lake—until now.

The other problem was the landscape. The earthquake had drastically rearranged the land. Roads had become canyons or small mountains. Maneuvering around the broken ground was time-consuming at best, treacherous at worst. Over time, by trial and error, Ben had learned how to get to nearby towns, but, as he recalled his trip from Washington, DC to Fontana Lake, and the time it took him to travel 500 miles, trial and error wouldn't work for long trips. For the same reason, even bicycles were of no use. No, wherever they decided to go, they'd have to walk.

They were in no rush. Time had long ago ceased to be important to them. The only factor was the weather. Depending on their destination, winter might become a stumbling block in the scenario.

They spent the next few days planning. They caught fish for food, saving some of their more portable food for the trip. Lila had also swooped through and picked some vegetables at the last minute before the fire. Food wasn't an immediate problem.

A more pressing issue was Lila's comfort level with using her left eye for shooting. They had a lot of ammunition—more than they could ever take with them—so target practice for both of them became a priority. Ben was never the marksman with guns that Lila had become. His expertise was with his crossbow. The practice with the guns would do him good.

For Lila, it was school all over again. Her skill at shooting a rifle from the right side was history. It felt to her as if she was handling a rifle for the first time. The pistols weren't too much of a problem with her left hand, as she had always practiced with both hands, but the rifle was another story.

Her first attempt at shooting was a disaster. She spent an hour sighting and dry-firing the rifle before using ammunition. They used a large piece of blackened plywood as a target, and set it up fifty feet away. She aimed and shot. The board didn't move.

She lowered the rifle and looked at Ben. "Where did it go?"

"Beats the heck out of me," answered Ben.

Lila started laughing and Ben breathed a sigh of relief, happy that Lila's sense of humor had returned. It seemed to him that she had already moved beyond the destruction of their home.

"Good thing we have a lot of ammunition," said Lila. "I'm going to need it."

Lila spent the rest of the day practicing. It was obvious that it was going to take some time, though.

There was a determination to Lila that I hadn't seen in a very long time. It was as if she was trying to exorcise the demons that had consumed her for so long, almost as if she knew she had wasted months of her life wallowing in her misery and now had to prove her worth. Whether she was trying to prove it to me or to herself didn't matter. She wouldn't quit until she had regained the shooting skill she had once been so proud of.

A few days later, Lila finally reached a point of comfort with her rifle, and Ben could tell she was anxious to get on the road.

He wasn't as ready as Lila, though. They hadn't seen anyone else in a long time. What had the world outside become. Had the electricity come back? Were people kinder to each other? Were they working together. Was there some order in the world?

He wanted to stay positive, but Ben couldn't help the dark thoughts from coming through. What if things had only gotten worse?

Chapter 3

Decisions had to be made. They could only carry so much, and much of it had to be ammunition, which was heavy. It had been six years since they had been anywhere further than the towns in the general vicinity of Fontana Dam, and a few years since they had seen another human.

We had no idea what to expect. Had towns become populated again? I was pretty sure they weren't, but what about stores? Had everything been cleaned out over the years? During our journey right after the event, supplies—including ammunition—were readily available. We couldn't be guaranteed of that anymore.

They knew they could live off the land, so using valuable space in their packs for food wasn't necessary. Instead, in addition to the ammunition, they loaded them with clothes and camping gear. Even Katie had her own pack.

I was blown-away by how well Katie was handling the whole situation. Back when I was a kid, I would have been whining at every juncture—the work, the discomfort, the uprooting, and even the acrid smell, the aftermath of the fire, still hanging in the air. Not Katie. That wasn't to say she wasn't sad about leaving the only home she ever knew, but living in the woods her whole life had made her adaptable. The violent weather could change plans quickly, as could the unexpected appearance of a bear or a cougar. No, what bothered Katie the most was the disappearance of the animals. Whether they escaped the fire or perished in it, they were gone. We had no worries about Katie. Maybe she could even teach us a thing or two about adaptability.

They stayed on the beach in front of their burned-out cabin for another three days before they felt ready to embark on their move to … to where? They had many discussions about their future and had finally decided to head southwest toward the Gulf of Mexico. If someone had asked them why they chose that area, they weren't sure they could tell them. It was more a process of elimination. Washington wasn't an option. As much as the new government might have been able to create a viable society there, the thought of living in a city after all this time was just too depressing for them. Florida was a similar situation. They wanted to live near the water, but most of the Florida coastline had been built-up. Again, too much city.

They considered going back from where they had originally come—to New England—but it would be too cold.

The accelerated climate change had brought more cold weather to their home in the Smokies, so they could only imagine what it was like up north. The southwest seemed the logical choice. Neither one of them had been to the panhandle of Florida or the Mississippi, Louisiana, or Texas coast. There had to be some communities there. If not, they could venture into New Mexico or Arizona. While those areas wouldn't have the ocean, they would be new and different. Their old friends Nick and Jason had told them that the west had been devastated by the earthquakes, but maybe somehow the earthquakes created as much as they destroyed—new vistas or new land masses. All they could do was to start walking. But as they discovered on their first trip years earlier, sometimes decisions were made for them.

*****

They picked a sunny day for their departure. The sky was a dark blue with almost no clouds. They had noticed over the last couple of years how brilliant the sky had become. Man-made pollution had come to a screeching halt, and the planet seemed to be healing itself. Or maybe it was just their imagination. Could the planet heal so quickly?

As they cast off the boat and headed to the center of Fontana Lake, they looked back at their former home in silence, each of them—even Katie—deep in thought. They were leaving a lot of memories. Ben was nervous for the trip. He recalled feeling some of the same fear when he and Lila first left their home in Massachusetts—two teenagers with no clue of what the future would bring and scared out of their minds. At least this time they had the skills and the experience to do what needed to be done. But still, the unknown was a scary place.

They docked at the dam and made their way up to the parking lot. Ben looked with fondness at his old truck, now rusting away from inactivity. So much of their first couple of years there had been spent collecting needed supplies and transporting them in the truck. Ben wasn't sad when he'd had to retire it due to lack of gas. They had reached a point where it was no longer necessary to stock up in the towns. They had all they needed at the cabin. He was sad now though, as if he was saying goodbye to an old friend.

The Appalachian Trail, their route for most of their trip south, was no longer of use to them. They needed to head more southwest, and decided to take whatever small roads would eventually lead them to the Cherohala Skyway through the mountains of Tennessee. From the map, it seemed a logical choice, but Ben knew from experience that the road might not even exist anymore. Everything about this trip was going to be on the fly, but they weren't worried. They had no schedule to keep, and it wasn't like they were taking Katie out of her element. She grew up in the woods. It was where she was most comfortable.

The first couple of days of their journey were uneventful. They hiked through the forests—some areas were untouched by the earthquake, and in others the landscape had totally shifted—and occasionally they found roads that were still relatively intact. The fire hadn't spread in that direction, so they were able to find animals and plants for food. The second night, they camped by the shores of a lake and dined on fish.

Ben and Lila were both impressed by Katie's fortitude. She

rarely complained, even though her backpack—small as it was—must have been heavy for her. It was Ben and Lila who were having the most trouble getting used to the walk. Their packs were heavy, and it had been a few years since they had last had to hike with packs.

At one point, Ben looked over at Lila. She was wiping away sweat from around her eye patch. Her limp was noticeable.

"Like old times?"

She laughed. "Sure. Except for the one eye, the aching ankle, the child, and the dog." She adjusted her rifle attached to her backpack. "Everything else feels all too familiar."

Their third day, they came upon a town. Katie stared in wonder. She hadn't been in a town since she was very young, and didn't remember it, so it was all new to her. After marveling at the buildings, many of them burned out, and the rusty abandoned cars, she pointed to one of the dozens of skeletons on the sidewalks. "Why are there so many?" she asked.

When Ben and Lila had made their journey, bodies were still decomposing. It had been a gruesome sight and flies were everywhere. After seven years, all that remained were the bones and clothes fragments.

"Do you remember us talking about what happened to the world?" Ben asked. Katie nodded. "These are some of the people who died. We are going to see a lot of them, so don't let it scare you."

"I'm not scared." And Ben knew she wasn't. She was more curious. She had seen a lot of animal bones in her life. In some way, this wasn't too different. The impact of the skeletons was felt more strongly by Ben and Lila. In their little corner of the world in the cabin by the lake, they had escaped all of this. Once they had ended their trips to towns, the obscenity caused by those in power could be forgotten. No longer.

I think we both felt more emotion than we thought we would. It wasn't a sadness for the individuals lying there in the streets. Maybe it should have been. I don't know. It was more of a sadness for mankind in general. How could we have done this to ourselves? We had societies that took centuries to form. They weren't perfect. Far from it. They were dysfunctional, and even dying in some respects, but they were who we were. There were brilliant aspects to our societies and there were parts that displayed our sheer stupidity. Good or bad, it was what we had created. And in one quick second it was gone. I could look at individual piles of bones and wonder: who were they, where were they going when it all ended, and would they have done anything differently with their lives if they had known what was coming? But those were just curiosities. No, the sadness took on a larger dimension. Maybe it was the result of one misguided man, but in reality, we were all to blame. We all helped bring down our planet, and most people had paid the ultimate price.

Ben was having second thoughts about their move. Would they have been better off finding something in another part of the forest? Did they really want to see what had become of the world? He looked at Lila, who glanced back. Ben could tell she was having similar thoughts. They were in the mountains now and knew they would run across just the occasional town.

What would happen when they emerged from all of that and reached suburbia and cities? Could they face it? Even when they were on their first journey, they stuck to the Appalachian Trail, so nature had been a major part of their life together from the very beginning.

What kinds of people—if any—would they encounter? And then he had the thought that Katie had never seen another human being. When she was very young, their friends Nick and Jason had shown up and stayed with them for a month, but she would never remember that.

Ben was just about to mention that to Lila, when, two blocks away a man appeared. He was pulling a cart of some kind, and he was walking toward them.

Chapter 4

He saw them, but kept on coming without a break in his stride. He had a pronounced limp.

"Is limping the new fad?" asked Lila, trying to inject some humor into a tense situation.

Katie slowly moved behind Lila, holding onto her leg. It was the first sign of timidity Ben had ever seen in Katie, but this was a completely new experience for her. Ben knew it wouldn't take her long to see that there was nothing to be afraid of ... he hoped, anyway.

As they approached each other, now less than a block away, Ben could hear the man singing. He couldn't make out the words, but it was a gentle song, a song you might sing to someone who was frightened. Was it for their benefit?

Taking nothing for granted, Ben and Lila both undid the straps on their holsters, freeing up their pistols.

When they were about fifty feet apart, they all stopped. Metal was clanging lightly in his now motionless wagon. It was nothing more than a garden-style wagon with extra-large wheels. Ben had sometimes seen similar things while on vacation at the beach on Cape Cod. The man had fashioned a cover that was reminiscent of a covered wagon from the old west.

"Howdy," he said. He was probably in his late-50s, a little stooped over, but with muscular arms and legs. His skin was leathery, with a dark tan, the result of years spent outdoors. He had a gray mustache that hung over his upper lip, and a scraggly beard that stopped below his Adam's Apple. Balding on top, what hair he did have was various shades of gray and secured in a ponytail down to his shoulder blades. He turned his head and spat a stream of brown juice on the road, wiping his mouth with his sleeve. A light breeze was blowing a ripe odor from him their way. Ben glanced down at Katie and saw her holding her nose.

"Hey," replied Ben.

"Don't see many folks anymore," the man said. A slight southern accent? Ben wasn't sure.

"We don't either," said Ben. Like for the last six years, he thought.

"Name's Frederick."

"I'm Lila. This is Ben, and this is Katie." Katie had inched out from Lila, but was still pinching her nose. "And that's Ralph," she said. Ralph was sitting right next to Katie, ready to protect her.

"Heard of you," said Frederick. "Not for a long time. Thought you were dead."

Six years after we disappeared from the scene, our exploits were still remembered. It wasn't like anything we did was monumental. Maybe it was just unusual to find people at that time who fought to live and fought for others. So many had given up. I know we offered hope to many that it was still possible to survive the apocalypse that had ravaged the world. Maybe that hope had reached further than we thought.

"Not dead," Ben answered. "We just got away from it all."

"Fire drive you out? Saw the smoke. Could smell it."

"It did," answered Lila. "It was time to leave anyway. We're heading southwest, toward the Gulf."

"Wouldn't suggest it." He spat again, and Ben could see his brown teeth.

"Why?"

"It's not there, 'least not the way it used to be."

Ben was about to respond when Frederick said, "Mind if I sit? Leg acts up."

"Of course," said Lila.

He walked over to a bench, currently occupied by what was left of a skeleton of a woman wearing a faded and torn flowered dress. He picked her up gently, many of the bones clattering to the ground, and laid what remained of her down next to the bench, then he sat down in her spot and motioned for Lila to sit beside him.

"Saw your limp," said Frederick. "Figured you could use a rest too."

She sat, trying hard to ignore the smell. Ben sat down in the street in front of them, Katie in his lap. Ralph had relaxed and was now exploring.

"Do you have a last name?" asked Ben, more as a conversation opener than actual curiosity.

"Do I need one anymore?"

I liked him. In the old days he might have been considered on the fringe of society. Now we all were. There was only the fringe. Or, we were the society. The line had been obscured.

"You were from up north somewhere, if I heard the story right."

"Massachusetts," answered Ben. "How about you?"

"Nashville."

"What were you singing when we saw you?" asked Lila. "It was pretty."

"Annie's Song, by John Denver. Always had a soft spot for that song. Had a dog named Annie."

Ben and Lila looked at each other, each shrugging their shoulders.

"Never heard the song?" he asked.

"Never heard of John Denver," answered Ben.

Frederick just shook his head.

"What was your job before all of ...?" Lila motioned around her.

"Homeless. I was one of those guys with a shopping cart." He laughed—it was more of a cackle. "Who would have thought that I'd be the one most prepared for this?"

"What did you mean that the Gulf coast isn't there?" asked Ben.

"Earthquake did it. Rearranged things. A lot of things. Had a lot of time to see for myself. Florida's under water. Texas, Mississippi, Louisiana, all of 'em, lost their coastline. Have a new coastline, but it's now cliffs and broken land. No beaches. Suppose some beaches will eventually form, but not like what used to be there."

"And Florida is gone?"

"Oh yeah. It was so low, the water just washed over it."

"What about the rest of the country?" asked Lila.

"Pretty beat up. Cities flattened—that's not such a bad thing, considering—mountains, crevasses, you name it."

"I saw a lot of that when I had to walk from Washington," said Ben.

Frederick's eyes grew wide and he withdrew into the bench. "When were you there?" It was a hoarse whisper.

"Six years ago," answered Ben. He cocked his head. "Why?"

Frederick relaxed. "Oh, six years ago. That's okay. You didn't hear?"

"We haven't heard anything. We've been off the grid for the last six years. We haven't left our home. You're the first person other than us that Katie has ever met."

"Then pull up a chair, boys and girls, 'cuz you've got a lot to learn." He was about to spit, but realized that Lila was on one side of him, the remains of the woman on the other, and Ben and Katie in front of him. He stood up, walked a few paces, then spat out his tobacco. He used his finger to clean out what was left in his gums, wiped his hands on his pants, then sat down again.

"Bout two, maybe three years ago, the plague hit. I call it

the plague—heard others use that term too—but I don't know
what it was. Disease of some kind. Places that had large
established communities got hit hard. A big one outside
Atlanta completely wiped out, Charlotte the same. Don't know
about northern cities."

"And Washington?" asked Ben.

"Gone."

Ben felt dizzy. His months imprisoned there had been
some of the worst of his life, mainly because he was separated
from Lila while she was pregnant with Katie. But he had
managed to make some friends. Dan and Gordon, friends he
and Lila had met earlier along the trail, had decided to stay
there. Colonel—now President—Jeffries was doing a good job
trying to rebuild the government. Even Brian, who saved Ben
on his way out of the city, when three assholes were about to
kill him. All gone? It was all too much to absorb.

"You don't know what the disease was?" asked Lila.

"People got sick and died," Frederick responded. "Don't
care what name they give it. Died fast, too, from what I heard."

"So some people survived?" asked Lila.

"Here and there. Didn't let them get too close to me. Some
of it I heard from a couple of queers I ran into. Nice guys."

"Nick and Jason?"

"That's them. Hey," he leaned toward Lila, the stench
making her pull back, "I don't judge people's lifestyles.
'Course, there ain't many people left to judge. Ha! And those
that are left sure don't have a lifestyle anymore." He gave a
cackle, finding himself funny.

Ben looked at Lila. "They're still alive."

"I would have thought," began Lila, "that if disease was

going to spread, it would have been right after the event, not four or five years later."

"There was some of that, too, early on. But they nipped it quick. This was something different. Even your friends there, as smart as they were, didn't know what it was. They figured it mighta started from one of those research labs. Maybe someone found something and let it out by mistake. Like that Ebola shit." He looked at Katie. "Sorry."

"No problem," said Ben, smiling.

"Anyways," Frederick continued. "The cities are prob'ly okay now, but I steer clear. Suggest you might want to, as well."

"Good advice," said Lila. "I guess we're going to have to change our plans."

"Hard to b'lieve the earthquake went that far west," said Frederick, "but it did."

"Nick told us that it was actually three quakes," explained Ben. "First the west coast ..." He momentarily thought of his brother, a Marine stationed at Camp Pendleton, most likely dead from the initial event. There hadn't been many people left alive to experience the earthquakes. "Then the Midwest, then finally here in the east. So I guess the whole country looks like that."

"Have you heard of any communities not affected by the plague?" asked Lila.

"I'm sure there's some. None I've run across. Heard a rumor coupla times—once from your friends, once from someone else I met a few months ago. Maybe it's just a rumor though. You know how they get started. Anyways, heard tell of a pretty big community spread out in Yellowstone. Really tryin' to make it work is what I heard."

Lila looked at Ben. "If it's true, something like that could be ideal. Contact with others, but with our own space." She turned to face Frederick. "If you had to guess, how accurate do you think the story is?"

He shrugged. "It's all a crapshoot these days. What can you believe. Story about you two is that you rid the country of about a hundred or hundred-fifty vermin. How accurate is that?" Ben knew he was fishing for information. The guy was lonely and needed a new story to tell the next people he encountered.

"I get your point," answered Ben. Frederick looked disappointed at the lack of information, so Ben felt he had to follow up. "Nowhere near that many. It just seemed like it to us."

Now that Frederick was mildly appeased, he offered more information. "Your friends there, Nick and Jason, I think they were convinced it existed, if that means anything."

It did.

"Has any power come back on?" asked Ben.

"From where?" responded Frederick incredulously. "Mighta had a chance after the apocalypse, depending on if there was anyone smart enough left to get it going. But then the earthquake—or quakes, as you say—hit. I 'spect that destroyed the power grid. Then the plague hit the cities. If anything was going on, that's where it woulda been happening. Maybe somewhere someone's got some makeshift power going. You ask me? That's all we're ever going to have."

The sun was starting to sink below the line of hills, so they felt it was time to move on and find a place to stay for the night. They had had enough of Frederick's smell. Besides, they knew he wouldn't want to camp with them. He had spent much of his life alone. He wouldn't want to change that now.

"We should be off," said Lila, thankfully moving away from the odor. "Thank you so much for the information."

"My pleasure. Thanks for the company." He glanced at Lila's rifle on her backpack. "From the stories I hear, you can use that pretty well." He pointed to the eye patch. "Still good with it?"

"Had to make some adjustments, but yeah, I am," she answered. Ben liked her strategy. If Frederick spread the news that he had seen them, better it be known that they were still capable of defending themselves.

"Reason I asked is that you might need it. Gangs of marauders here and there. Three, four in a group. Sometimes as many as six. Pretty much leave me alone these days. Take what they need from my wagon, then go. Don't think they'd be as accommodating to you." He was speaking directly to Lila, the implication clear.

"Thanks," said Ben. "We'll keep our eyes open."

"Somethin' else. Heard another rumor. Another group out west—not Yellowstone, someplace else—somethin' bad goin' on."

"Bad in what way?"

"Don't know. It's all just rumors. Everything to me is just rumors. They say it's evil—the worst kind of evil. Never met anyone who knows any more than that, but folks are scared. Maybe nothin' to it. Just thought I'd tell you."

"Thanks for the heads up," said Ben. "We'll ask people if we see any. You take care."

"Always do." He limped off, with the tinkling in his wagon and his odor both lingering.

Yellowstone. It would take us many months to get there, but there was something hopeful about it. I knew Lila felt the same way. We'd never get there by winter, though, so we'd have to find a place along the way to hunker down. Were we up for the trip? And what if the rumor of the community was unfounded. Could we deal with the disappointment? We had no choice really. It seemed our best option. Yellowstone it was.

Chapter 5

They made it another three miles before finally settling down for the night in a secluded copse of trees. Heeding Frederick's warning about the marauders, they decided to hold off building a fire, eating some leftover fish from the night before.

Ben watched as Katie ate her meal seemingly without a care in the world. He marveled at her adaptability, but at the same time felt a touch of sadness. The world that he grew up in was far from perfect, but he wished Katie could have experienced it. She would be starting first grade. They would have done their school shopping, picking out clothes, crayons, and other supplies. In some ways that life seemed so long ago, but when he watched Katie, it brought it all back as if it was yesterday. A lump formed in his throat.

"She'll be fine."

Ben turned to look at Lila. How did she know what he was thinking?

"Don't you ever wish ..." He didn't need to finish the sentence.

"Sometimes, but it does us no good to wish for the past. Katie never experienced it, so she doesn't miss it. Look at her." Katie had her head on a sleeping Ralph's belly. She yawned. "She's happy. For us, it's all been too surreal. For her, it's the most natural thing in the world. If we try to impose our memories on her—even if just in our own minds—we're not being fair to her. And it just makes us sad. This is the life we've been handed. At times it's sucked," she fingered her patch, "and at times it's been beautiful. No different from our old life in that respect. We accepted that this is how it is a long time ago. Let's not get sad about it now."

"Maybe it's just the fact that we're on the move again," said Ben. "It brings back memories."

Lila leaned over and put a blanket over the now passed out Katie, then snuggled in close to Ben. "Let's think about where we're going. Even if the Yellowstone community doesn't exist, it might be a good place to settle back down. Similar to where we were, but different."

They fell asleep in each other's arms.

*****

They were on the road early the next morning, buoyed by the knowledge that for much of Tennessee they would be able to mostly avoid towns. There was still a lot of wilderness. They stuck to the small back roads, following the compass that Ben had finally mastered a few years earlier, to make sure they were maintaining a northwesterly direction.

They came across small towns from time to time, but most were heavily overgrown. The earthquake had caused cracks in much of the concrete, and over the years weeds, grasses, and flowers had grown tall, oftentimes obscuring storefronts and houses—or what was left of them after the earthquakes and fires. It was as if nature had suddenly been freed from its concrete prison and was celebrating that freedom to the extreme.

Suddenly they weren't wary of encountering towns. Ben remembered pictures he had seen of hidden pyramids in Mexico and Central America, overgrown to the point where people could pass right by without seeing them.

The thriving vegetation served another purpose. Skeletons were hidden from view, the reminders of the past disappearing altogether. Occasionally they would find towns that had less growth, such as the one in which they met Frederick, but those were rare. America was slowly returning to its wild roots, and Ben couldn't be happier.

Wildlife was abundant and not a day went by when they didn't see deer, bears, rabbits, and raccoons, not to mention farm animals—herds of wild cattle and sheep, and the occasional horse. Birds of all colors and sizes flew by all day long. There were times when they felt they were on a different planet from the one they once occupied.

But then there were the dogs. A threat right after the cataclysmic events of so many years ago, dog packs were even more prevalent now. For the most part they kept their distance, but Ben and Lila knew that they could attack at any time. To his credit, Ralph stayed close to Katie, always on guard.

The going was sometimes tough. As Ben remembered from his grueling walk from Washington to Fontana Lake, the terrain was uneven, often forcing them to go miles out of their way to find level ground or to avoid great cracks in the earth. But as long as they kept bearing northwest, they knew they'd be fine. They took frequent breaks, mostly to allow Katie to rest her short legs. But Ben knew that Lila also appreciated the breaks to give her ankle some comfort. Late in the day her limp would became slightly more pronounced, but she pushed on without complaint.

Lila was amazing. The ankle was one thing, but it was her damaged eye that must have bothered her more. I knew that she had become accepting of her loss of vision, but it must have been so frustrating for her. She spent a lot of time turning her head to the right to try to get a full view. Lila would never want me to feel sorry for her, but sometimes I couldn't help it.

They walked another two days before encountering their first problem. They went through numerous towns, each time marveling at how little they resembled anything familiar. Then they realized that the route to Yellowstone would take them through the open spaces of the Midwest. The miles and miles of concrete that was the east coast was a thing of the past.

When trouble came, it was in the form of one of the marauding gangs they had been warned about. Ben had shot a wild turkey and they were making camp for the night. They took a chance on a fire in order to cook the turkey. Bigger than they needed, the bird would provide meals for several days. It was close to being ready, with the aroma filling the air, when they heard a rustling in the bushes. Ralph stood in front of

Katie and growled menacingly in the direction of the sound.

"Hello the fire," came a voice. "I'm friendly. Can I come in?"

"With your arms spread," answered Ben. He and Lila both had a bad feeling. Lila inched her rifle close to her and slipped her pistol onto her lap.

A lone man stepped into the clearing, his hands well clear of his holster. Strapped to his back was a worn rifle.

"I'm friendly," he repeated. Ben knew he was anything but. He was thin, bordering on gaunt, and looked to be about Ben's age, so he, too, would have been a teenager when it all happened. He kept glancing over at the turkey as he approached. Ben wondered if his friends were just as hungry.

"Smelled your food. Was wondering if you'd mind sharing a bit."

"Have a seat," answered Ben. The others were obviously sizing up the situation before making their move. The stranger sat down on the ground and Ben moved closer. He whispered to their guest, "I have a gun pointed at your gut. My wife has a gun pointed at your gut. You will be gutless in about ten seconds unless you call to your friends and tell them that everything is good and to come in with their hands empty."

"It's only m...."

"One ... two ... three ..."

"You can come in," he called nervously. "These people are okay. No need for guns."

Three others came out of the shadows. The oldest was barely thirty, the youngest still a teenager. The third looked remarkably like their guest. A brother, thought Ben. Maybe even a twin. They were all thin.

And they were all carrying rifles.

"Tell them," whispered Ben.

"You can put your guns away."

They visibly relaxed and as they did, Ben and Lila both jumped up and pointed their guns at the quartet. One tried to raise his rifle.

"Don't," shouted Ben. "I don't want to kill you, but I will if I have to." Lila cocked her pistol to add emphasis.

"What the fuck?" exclaimed the brother. "Dave, you said it was okay."

"He had a gun pointed at my stomach. What the fuck else was I going to say?"

"Pile your weapons over there," said Ben, "then take a seat."

Slowly, the group complied.

When they were all on the ground, Ben said, "We're friendly people. As you can see, we're a family. But we've killed more people than we can count, so don't misjudge us. Now, you guys look hungry and we're willing to share our food with you. We have nothing else of value, so we're not worth robbing—not that you could—so consider this a time-out from your usual activities. Got it?"

The youngest one was staring at Lila. "I know you," he said. "A long time ago. You were sitting by a trail. I was with a small group—a couple of women and a couple of guys older than me. You warned us that the men who were killing a bunch of people were nearby. You told us to keep heading south. You didn't have the eye patch then, but I remember you. Your name is Lila."

Lila remembered the incident as if it was yesterday. Right

after that, she had killed three of the men he was referring to—all former prisoners. The day before, the gang had murdered a whole community of people—men, women, and even children. Lila remembered it too well.

"Lila?" asked Dave. "As in Ben and Lila?" Ben nodded. "We heard you were dead."

"A common misconception," said Lila.

"I'm Mac." The younger one turned to the rest. "Hey, they're okay. I might not be alive if it wasn't for her."

"What happened to the rest of your group?" asked Lila.

"No idea. I didn't really know them anyway. I was only with them a few more days, then I hooked up with another group. Most of them died. I drifted after that."

How common a story was that? Kids who should have been playing video games from the comfort of their bedrooms drifting from group to group, hoping for a little stability in their lives. Everyone who survived the event had a different story to tell. The one constant though was the search for some sort of family. I had a feeling these four would always be searching.

The turkey was done, so Ben ripped it apart, giving the larger pieces to their new "friends." The four ate hungrily. The marauder business had obviously seen better days. Nobody talked, the four too focused on filling their stomachs. Ben and Lila didn't think they'd turn on them at this point, but they kept their guns close anyway.

"How many people you kill?" asked Dave.

What was the fascination with the number of people who had died at our hands? I was beginning to wonder exactly what the rumors were about us. You'd think we were a two-person army.

"Enough," I answered.

"I killed a man once," said Dave.

Ben said nothing.

Dave's brother poked him. "Shut up, Dave."

"Knock it off, Richie. I was just saying."

Ben and Lila looked at each other, the same memory coming to mind. Richie was the name of the manager of the restaurant they worked for when the event happened. A particularly unpleasant individual, he thought he was punishing them by having them do inventory in the walk-in freezer. In reality, his sleaziness saved them. When the EMP hit, it was the freezer that protected them. Richie's lifeless body was lying right outside the door when they emerged.

"Where're you coming from?" asked Richie.

"We were living in the forest a ways back," answered Lila. "Fire forced us out. We're heading west."

"Wouldn't suggest it." The oldest of the foursome finally spoke.

"Why?" asked Ben.

"You hear things, is all."

"What kinds of things?"

"Things. Not a healthy place to be."

"Are you talking about the evil?" asked Lila.

"Guess you could call it that."

"Do you know what it is?"

"Nope. Don't have any desire to find out. Ran into people, different people, all said the same thing. Just happy to get out alive. No one would tell us what it was. 'People' was all they'd say."

"Hear anything about a community in Yellowstone?" asked Ben.

"Heard rumors."

"Ever thought to check it out?"

"Thought about it. Not worth it. Have to go through 'them' to get there. Rather stay here."

Were we going to hear anything more than rumors? The evil was a rumor. The Yellowstone community was a rumor. It was a big country with a very few people. Maybe rumors were the best we were going to get.

"You're welcome to bed down here for the night," said Lila. "But we'll hold onto your guns 'til morning. Or you can leave and come back tomorrow for the guns. Either way, we keep the guns for the night. Hope you can understand."

"We understand," said the older guy. "We'd do the same. No hard feelings. Stay here, if you don't mind. We're tired. Truth be told, this was the first good meal we've had in a while. Animals all over the place. Just haven't had any luck."

Ben stoked the fire while everyone got comfortable. Silence descended on the camp.

Katie still hadn't talked to anyone other than Ben and Lila. They knew it would take a while for her to get comfortable. They hoped that by the time they reached the community in Yellowstone—if it really existed—she'd be ready to talk to others.

Katie crawled into Lila's arms and the two drifted off. Their four "guests" were also falling asleep—two were already snoring. Ben moved over to a tree next to the pile of guns. Ralph came over and curled up next to him. Ben knew that if he dozed off, Ralph would wake him if something was wrong. But he wouldn't doze. It was going to be a long sleepless night.

Chapter 6

They said goodbye to their new friends early the next morning and were on their way. While he trusted them to an extent, Ben still watched them until they were out of sight, now that they had their weapons back. He hoped they could talk their way out of the next encounter with wandering marauders just as easily. About a mile into the walk, they stopped at a stream to fill their canteens. All the death had come so long ago, they felt they could trust streams and lakes to have uncontaminated water. So far that had proven true.

They had just put their packs back on when they heard a growl. Ralph was staring into the underbrush crouched in an attack position. They heard rustling.

"Down, Ralph," said Lila quietly, all the while slowly unslinging her rifle from her backpack. Seeing her mother do that, Katie looked at Ben and said, "My crossbow, Daddy?"

As she had always done when they were hunting, Katie sensed the danger and she wanted to help. There was no question in Ben's mind what to do. He reached behind him and detached the smaller crossbow for his daughter. While only six, she had already proven herself while hunting. There was no sense in shielding her when she could be of help. He loaded the bolt into the crossbow and handed it to Katie. There was no need to tell her to be careful. She knew the rules of handling a weapon.

He was reaching for his rifle when a large dog shot out of the woods right at Katie. She screamed and dropped her crossbow, the suddenness of the attack startling her. Ralph jumped at the attacker and caught him in mid-air, the two hitting the ground heavily. As they landed, three more dogs burst from the trees and ran toward them. Lila got a shot off and dropped one ten feet from her. Ben took a quick shot, missed, then shot again, this time grazing a large German Shepherd. It rolled for a moment, then came to its feet to continue the attack. Lila shot and hit it in the neck, throwing it a half a dozen feet, where it lay dead. The third one came up on Lila's blindside and hit her hard. Not being able to prepare for it, she went down, dazed. The dog jumped on top of her, about to go for her throat.

"Mommy!" cried Katie.

Ben pulled out his pistol and shot three times, being ever so careful not to hit Lila. The dog limped away and Ben shot again. This time the dog crumpled to the ground, unmoving. He heard the sudden "thwap" of a crossbow and looked down to see Katie lowering her weapon. The dog Ralph had attacked was lying on the ground with the shaft of a bolt protruding from its side. Ralph had gotten the worse of the fight, and was lying on the ground, bloody.

That seemed to be the end of the dog pack. No others

appeared.

"Good job, Katie," said Ben. "You check on Ralph while I look after Mommy."

Lila was bleeding from a head wound, a deep scratch on the neck, and a puncture wound in her shoulder, but she was conscious.

"God, I'm a mess," she said, attempting to smile.

"Just lie back." He reached for his backpack and found a bar of soap and a small towel. He showed her. "Best I can do," he said, but she had passed out.

He poured water on the towel and lathered it up, then proceeded to clean the wounds, happy that Lila wasn't awake.

"How's Ralph, Kiddo?" he asked.

Katie looked up at him with tears in her eyes. "He's hurt, Daddy. I don't want him to die."

"I'll look at him just as soon as I fix Mommy."

Katie looked scared. "Is Mommy going to be okay?" The tears were now flowing down her cheeks.

"She will. Don't you worry." He just wished he could be as confident about Ralph. He finished washing Lila, then got some clean bandages from Lila's backpack and wrapped her wounds. Once he was confident that she was comfortable, he saw to Ralph.

Ben had had to fix Ralph up a number of times over the years when he got into fights with other animals, but this was the worst he had seen. A large piece of skin on his leg had flapped back, revealing a deep wound. He had other bite marks and scratches, but the leg was the thing that concerned Ben the most.

He worked on Ralph for almost an hour, taking moments

off to check on Lila. Ralph must have been in excruciating pain, but he trusted Ben implicitly. Even so, when Ben touched a particularly raw spot, Ralph would give a yelp. All the time, Katie alternated between Ralph and Lila, stroking their heads and telling them they'd be okay.

Finally, Ben could do no more. He made sure each of his patients was warm and in the shade, then he scrubbed the dirt and blood off himself in the stream. When he was clean, he sat with Katie under a tree.

"I'm very proud of you," he said to his daughter, who was leaning up against him.

"I had to shoot that dog," she answered. "He was hurting Ralph."

"You did the right thing. And," he mussed her hair, "you've become a really good shot. But it's not just that that I'm proud of you for. You shot that dog because you were protecting Ralph, just like he tried to do for you. And you did that while being scared. That's not an easy thing. I love you, Kiddo."

"I love you too, Daddy." And she was asleep, worn out from the stress, the fear, and the adrenaline rush.

Ben knew they weren't going anywhere for a while.

*****

They stayed by the stream for over a week. Lila was up and around the next day, although sore and moving gingerly, but Ralph's wounds were more severe. As anxious as they were to get going, Ralph's needs were just as important as their own. After a couple of days, they felt a sense of relief when Ralph turned the corner and it was apparent that his wounds were beginning to heal. It was Ralph, himself, who told them that he was ready to travel when he woke them up one morning standing in front of them with his tail wagging. They quickly packed their things and took to the road once more.

Ralph walked gingerly, but didn't seem to be in any real pain.

"Yet another gimp," joked Ben.

Lila punched him in the shoulder.

"Hope we get a bit further, this time," said Ben.

"If we continue at this rate, by the time we reach Yellowstone, they will all have died of old age," answered Lila.

They still couldn't believe how the landscape of the towns had changed. Not only had grass and weeds grown up through the cracks cause by the earthquake, trees were also coming up in force.

"Another twenty years and you won't be able to see the towns at all," Lila said as they passed a car with a young tree growing up through its rusted chassis and out the driver's side window.

"Not even sure it will take twenty years," replied Ben. "There is nothing to stop the growth. Nature is thriving and nothing is going to stop it."

"Why do you think everything is growing so fast?" asked Lila. "The constant rain storms?"

"Six years of that would do it, I would think. But I'm wondering if it's even greater than that. We're not here to hinder it. There's no one to pave over it or to spray it. The air seems to be clearing of pollution. It's been given the green light."

"What does that mean, Daddy?"

Lila looked at Ben. "Isn't it funny how so many of our old expressions mean nothing in this new world?"

They ran across a small town that had been spared the worst from the earthquake, and they decided to stock up on a few things. They entered a large department store. Some of the walls had crumbled and it was missing part of its roof, but even with that it was in better shape than most. All three needed new clothes, and Ben needed new boots. Katie looked around in awe at the shelves of clothes. She had never seen anything like it, and Lila decided to let her take her time and soak in the experience.

Ben quickly got bored in the clothing section and sought out the sporting goods department, picking out new sleeping bags for them all. He also selected a second compass and a new hunting knife.

When he and Lila made their first journey, freeze-dried meals would have been at the top of the list. Now, everything they ate came from the earth, or fresh meat that they killed. It wasn't worth the valuable space to carry freeze-dried food. He made his way over to a drug store, where he stocked up on bandages and soap. He opened a bottle of alcohol, but it had all evaporated. He did find some hydrogen peroxide that seemed okay, though long out of date. Anything else he found would also be so out of date, and as such, useless to them. That probably included condoms, as well. Ben wasn't about to take a chance on them. Besides, he hadn't used condoms for a few years, once they ran out. They had learned to make love according to Lila's cycles. He looked around him inside the drug store and realized how unnecessary so much of it all had become for them.

Ben met Lila and Katie in the street. Katie was wearing a SpongeBob t-shirt.

"She thought it was cute," said Lila.

"I miss SpongeBob," said Ben. "And Scooby-Doo. It would be fun to watch them again. Katie would love them."

"Maybe someday," answered Lila. "You never know. It's funny," she added, "Katie picked out a few Scooby-Doo t-shirts as well. Like father like daughter."

"I'm going to have to teach you the Scooby-Doo and SpongeBob songs," Ben said to his daughter. She gave him a puzzle expression.

"We told you a little bit about cartoons," explained Ben. "At the beginning of the cartoon was a song." He started singing, "Scooby Dooby-Doo, Where are you..." He stopped. Katie was laughing hysterically. He looked at Lila, who was laughing along with Katie. "I think we'll definitely have to teach her the songs."

They had had enough of the town. Even Katie had lost interest. The newness of the experience had already passed.

As they were leaving the outskirts, gunshots and yelling suddenly erupted. It was close. They crouched behind a car, guns drawn. They waited, but the shooting wasn't getting any closer, so they decided to keep moving, keeping close to the buildings.

They were across from a vacant lot when they saw the source of the shooting: a group of five men—similar in appearance to their guests of a week earlier, but older—had set up skeletons in a row and were using them as target practice. They weren't very good shots, and Ben realized quickly the source of the problem. They were all staggeringly drunk. Every time someone shot, the others would jeer at his bad aim and babble as to how much of a better shot they were.

It was disgusting. It wasn't the waste of precious ammunition or the fact that they were so drunk. It was the sheer disrespect they showed to those who were once living, breathing human beings. The skeletons were hung like scarecrows. Some had shattered skulls where a bullet had surprisingly hit its mark, and others had various bones blown away. There was something so sad about it, it brought tears to my eyes. I looked at Lila. There was no doubt she was feeling the same. I wanted so badly to go over and blow those guys away, but I refrained.

The group was so drunk, Ben and his family could have walked right past them and probably wouldn't have been seen, but they stayed hidden while they walked until they were out of view and earshot of the gang. They kept on, putting as many miles between them and the town as possible.

They set up camp in, appropriately enough, an old campground. It was on the shores of a small lake, so Ben and Katie went fishing for dinner while Lila started a fire. Ben was confident they'd come back with fish. The lakes and ponds were so populated these days that they were bound to catch a half a dozen within minutes.

An hour later Ben was grilling some good-sized fish over the fire. Lila had found what once was someone's garden, but had run wild over the years. Although most of the vegetables had died this late in the season, she still managed to come back with an armful of potatoes, tomatoes, and carrots.

They had just started their meal when Ralph growled.

"Oh, not again," whispered Lila, reaching for her rifle.

There was rustling in the overgrown forest beyond the camp site. It sounded different this time, though. Not dogs. It was almost clumsy, Ben thought.

"Hello?" came a man's voice. It was halting, like he was out of breath. "Can I approach?"

"Come in slowly," answered Ben. "Hands wide." It was almost déjà vu, he thought.

A man who looked to be in his thirties came into the clearing. The sun hadn't yet gone down, so they could get a good look at him. He had a well-kept beard peppered with flecks of gray. He was also scared. They both knew immediately that he was no marauder.

"Please," he said. "My wife is hurt. She needs help. We were attacked by dogs. They scattered all of our belongings. I have nothing to use to help her. Please?"

"Of course," said Lila. "Bring her in. Do you need help with her?"

"No, I can get her. Thank you so much."

They still had their old sleeping bags, so Lila put them down for the man's wife to lie on, then got the bag of items Ben had retrieved from the drug store. A few minutes later, they heard more crashing in the woods and the man emerged supporting his wife, who was covered in blood and barely conscious. By his side was a young girl, older than Katie, but not by a lot—maybe eight or nine.

"Set her down here," said Lila, motioning to the sleeping

bags. "Where is she hurt the worst?"

"The top of her head, I think. It's pretty bad." He was wringing his hands in distress. "Usually I know what to do, and I'm a lot calmer than this, but we don't have anything now, and … and …"

"Come over here," said Ben, interrupting. "Let Lila see to her." Lila had been motioning to Ben to distract the distraught husband.

"I'm Ben, and this is our daughter Katie."

"I'm Rob, and this is Amber." As he talked, he kept glancing back at Lila, who was washing the blood off to get a closer look at the wounds. "My wife is Jenny."

"What happened?"

"Dogs. A big pack. Six or eight of them. They must have smelled the venison in Jenny's backpack. They hit us so quickly we didn't even have time to draw our weapons. We tried to fight them off with sticks and whatever we had. Jenny was trying to get her pack off, but it was stuck, and they kept jumping on her to get to it. When she finally got it off, they ignored us and ripped at the pack. We just had to get as far away as possible. I was about to lay her down and try to find some water to wash her when I smelled the fish cooking."

All the while, Katie was staring at Amber.

"Why is she staring?" asked Amber.

"Katie has lived her whole life in the woods. She's never met another kid. You're the first one. I just think she's shy. Maybe you could talk to her. Maybe she won't be so shy around people then."

Lila motioned for Ben and Rob.

"Amber, stay with Katie, okay?" said Rob. "We'll be right

over here."

Katie looked at Ben, who nodded his approval, so she stayed sitting.

"I think Jenny has lost a lot of blood," said Lila when they moved over to her. "She seems to only have the one wound, but it's pretty ugly. The dogs almost scalped her. A large part of her scalp has come away from her head. But it's still attached to the rest of the scalp, so I think I can sew it. I've tried to wash it as best I can. I want to pour hydrogen peroxide on it. We don't know if it's still any good, but it's worth trying. It might hurt, so I'll need you to hold her. She goes in and out of consciousness. Maybe if we're lucky, she'll stay unconscious."

They weren't lucky. As soon as the peroxide hit the wound, Jenny screamed. It was long and loud, and then she passed out. Lila threaded a needle, sterilized it with a match and more of the hydrogen peroxide, and set to work stitching the wound. This time Jenny didn't wake up.

"It's just regular thread," said Lila. "But it's the best we have. Hopefully it will do the job."

"I can't tell you how much I appreciate all of this. She was losing so much blood, I don't know if she would have lived through it."

"I think we've all been there," said Ben. "I'm glad we were here to be able to help."

Rob cocked his head to the side. "You said your name is Ben, and that's Lila? The Ben and Lila? Most people think you're dead."

"Yeah, so we've heard."

"Do you know there's a song about you?"

"You're joking," Ben said with a laugh.

"I'm serious. There were so many stories about you, some musician somewhere came up with a song. I really don't know the words, but it has to do with you both suddenly appearing from nowhere and saving people. You helped people escape from a prison compound, and you rid the world of vermin. It has you arriving on a boat from a distant land."

"Yeah, Massachusetts … by foot, though. You know, I think many of the stories were exaggerated a hundred-fold. We were in the right place at the right time to help a number of people, but there were people we couldn't help. We're still haunted by that."

"Well, wherever the truth lies, the fact is, you became an inspirational couple to many people. The stories of you—however exaggerated—gave people hope, and God knows we all needed hope."

Katie and Amber still hadn't said anything to each other.

"Katie, it's okay to say hi." She moved over to Ben and snuggled next to him. "Well, maybe later," he said to her.

Looking at Rob, he said, "This is all very new to her. All she's ever known is Lila and me, and Ralph the dog. It's going to take some time. Where are you from?"

"Out west. Jenny is from South Carolina and really wanted to come home. I'm okay with it. We heard there was a small community near her hometown. She's hoping she'll know someone. We've been in Minnesota."

"Do you know anything about a community at Yellowstone?"

"I do. Never been there, but I've met people who have. It's good. I hear it's maybe a thousand people in all. They're spread out, but they built a small gathering place—I guess a town, of sorts—with a school and a church. The reports have been good."

"You didn't want to go there?"

"No, Jenny really wanted to go this way."

"We're headed for Yellowstone," said Ben.

Rob assumed a worried expression. He said quietly, "Then we'd better talk after the girls are in bed. Need to tell you some things. I don't know if you're going to want to make that trip."

Could it be the "evil" was finally going to be explained?

Chapter 7

Jenny still hadn't regained consciousness, but her breathing and pulse seemed normal, so Lila wasn't worried. While she slept, the other adults put the girls down. Not a word had yet been said between Katie and Amber. Ben and Lila gave Katie a kiss, and she was asleep in minutes. After the day Amber had had, she was right behind Katie in sleep.

Ben stoked the fire while Lila checked again on Jenny.

Rob looked over her shoulder as she changed the bandage on Jenny's scalp. There was a fair amount of leakage, and Lila had to change the dressing every couple of hours.

"How's she doing?" he asked.

"I did the best I could with what I had, but it's not going to heal pretty," answered Lila. "I know all about things like that," she added, pointing to her eye patch.

"How did it happen?" asked Rob.

They walked to the fire and sat down with Ben. She told Rob the story of the deer, which then transitioned into the story of their journey south and their six years in the cabin. When they were done, Rob took his turn and related his story.

He and Jenny, along with two-year-old Amber, were in the basement of a bank in Milwaukee checking their safe deposit box when the event hit. The stunned family and the bank employee spent a week walking the streets of Milwaukee, encountering a very few equally stunned survivors. Finally, common sense kicked in and Rob and Jenny came up with a plan. Rob had relatives near Minneapolis, and since that was closer than South Carolina, they made that their destination. The bank employee was still consumed by fear and didn't want to leave her home city. The last they saw of her, she had hooked up with a group of about eight equally shell-shocked individuals.

"I'm sure they were all dead within a couple of months," said Rob. "I don't think they had one rational mind among them."

Eventually they made it to Minneapolis. Of course, Rob's relatives were nowhere to be found. They joined up with about thirty others and formed a loose community—together mainly for the illusion of force, in case they encountered dog packs or bandits, as they called them. They lost ten of their group in the earthquake. Theirs was the second of the three quakes, the one originating on the Madrid fault. After six years in Minneapolis they finally got tired of the violent winter weather and decided to head south to Jenny's hometown.

"So Minneapolis wasn't hit by the plague?" asked Lila.

"No. Maybe the cold weather kept it away. I only found out about the plague last year. We've been on the road a few months," he finished. "And now," he said, looking at the anticipation in Ben's face, "you want to know about the 'evil', as I've heard it called."

Ben nodded.

"Most of the people who refer to the 'evil' have never experienced it. We haven't. So this is all second-hand—or maybe third-hand. It's a group, a big group, out to create their own empire. I don't know how they all found each other. Maybe they were already together and survived the event as a group. I have no idea. I do know that they take hostages—men, women, and especially children. Anyone they deem not strong enough, they abandon—often in places they will never survive in. They seem to have long-range plans—again, I don't know what they are. The group is based in western Nebraska, but sends searchers far and wide looking for communities to consume. I doubt if you'd find a viable community anywhere from Illinois to Montana. The rumor is that they won't touch the Yellowstone group. Maybe because they are too large and too strong? I don't know. But here's the thing. They have electricity—lots of it. They have gas and they have vehicles. That makes them very powerful."

"And their goal is to build an empire?" asked Lila.

"The information we got has been piecemeal. Some of those who talked to us were too scared to say much, and others just didn't know anything beyond what they had experienced. One guy we talked to was part of a small community in Iowa—fifteen or twenty people. One day the trucks swooped in—three of them—and rounded up all the residents. The guy said he was out hunting and came back just in time to see what was happening."

"Did he try to help?" Asked Ben.

"One guy against six heavily armed men? He knew he

didn't stand a chance. Besides, he had no family there, so he didn't have the motivation any of us would have. He said they just loaded everyone aboard the trucks and took off."

"Were they new trucks or old?" asked Ben.

"Don't know." He looked at Ben. "I know what you're thinking. That was the first thing that struck me. Have they found a way to repair the circuit boards? Can't tell you that, but they seem to be a fully functioning society. Just the fact that they have electricity means they've made some sort of progress." He turned to Lila. "To answer your question as best I can, I would say that their goal is to populate that society. I used the term 'empire'. That seems to be the best way to describe it. Of course, it wouldn't take much to form an empire out here. The remaining population seems to be even smaller than I imagined."

"Ben and I both had experiences with those kinds of people," said Lila, remembering her weeks of internment without Ben on their trip south.

"I heard about that," said Rob. "One of the people who joined our group in Minnesota had been in that camp and told us all about it. He said you were the inspirational leader and killed the head honcho. That was nothing compared to this, though. I bet over the last few years there have been dozens of attempts to build a new government—a new republic—mostly by people who only had their own needs in mind. This one is different. The motivations are the same as many of those others, but they are much better organized, are strong from the top down, and again, most of all, have the ability to turn the power back on."

"How do they get around the earthquake devastation?"

asked Ben. "The craters and canyons would make it almost impossible to go very far by truck."

"Don't know how. They just do it."

"They must have a leader," remarked Lila. "Any information on who it is?"

"Not a clue."

They were all silent for a minute, then Rob said, "Anyway, it's not safe out there. You never know where they're going to be. If they catch sight of you, they'll pick you up. This is the first time we've felt safe in a long time. I don't think they've come this far east yet. The Yellowstone community is a great goal, but it's going to be a dangerous trip, especially with a young girl. You need to think about it. If you change your mind, you're welcome to come with us to South Carolina."

The conversation stalled at that point, and they called it a night. Lila checked on Jenny, then she and Ben crawled into their sleeping bags next to Katie, while Rob did the same with his family.

Nothing was ever easy in this new world. There was always a tradeoff. We had a chance to start a new life in Yellowstone, but the dangers in getting there were extreme. I knew that it was important for Katie to grow up around other people, but I was already missing our life by the lake. We appreciated Rob's offer, but we were determined to go west. If it had just been Lila and me, there would be no inner conflict at all, but did we want to expose Katie to the danger the "evil" presented? Realistically though, was there anything in the new civilization that didn't present a danger? Would Rob's journey be any less hazardous than ours?

No, there was no question about it. We had to try.

Chapter 8

Their trip west was going molasses slow. Every time they got started, something would pop up to impede their progress. On one level it was frustrating, but on another, they knew they wouldn't reach Yellowstone before the winter even under the fastest circumstances, so they would just deal with the hand they were dealt. They stayed with Rob and his family for four days to allow Jenny to heal.

Two days after they met, Ben and Rob backtracked Rob's trail until they found the spot of the dog attack. After a couple of hours of searching, they were able to recover most of the scattered belongings, including all of their weapons.

Rob looked through a ripped backpack and said, "Jenny is going to be so happy. We had a few pictures and other mementos from our old life. They're still here. It would have killed her to lose them."

When they arrived back at the campsite, they found Jenny sitting up and eating some soup Lila had prepared. The smile on Rob's face when he saw her said it all. Ben was greeted with a surprise of his own. When he saw Lila, she put her finger to her lips and pointed to the edge of the woods. Amber and Katie were talking animatedly and playing together. Another bridge crossed.

Finally the time came to part ways. Seeing how much Katie and Amber had bonded almost made Ben and Lila change their minds and accompany Rob and family to South Carolina. But something was drawing them west. Who was to say that the plague that wiped out much of the east hadn't killed the settlement Rob and Jenny were hoping to find? The little they had heard about the Yellowstone settlement gave them hope. It sounded like the exact situation they were searching for—the ability to retain their privacy while still having contact with others. Their gut told them that the South Carolina settlement—if it existed—would not be what they were looking for. They had to listen to their inner leanings.

The goodbyes were tearful—oddly enough, Ben noticed, not for Katie and Amber. Had growing up in the new world made them more resilient? Could they adapt to change more easily? Maybe it was a very simple concept: they had enjoyed each other's company, but now it was time to go. Ah, thought Ben. If only the adults could learn something from that.

They traveled several days seeing no other people and no dog packs. At first they would check out town names against their atlas to know what state they were in, before coming to the realization that they really didn't care. States no longer existed. As long as they were going in the direction they wanted, they could start to use the towns later on to help with course adjustment.

The plant growth was staggering. It was as if in six years,

the country had gone back in time 300 years.

"It's like by breaking up the concrete, the earthquakes freed Mother Nature," said Lila in awe as they stood at the top of a ridge, looking down into a green valley. "She was a prisoner who was suddenly given the keys to her freedom, and she's going to make the most of it."

However, it didn't make for easy walking. Sometimes they found a stretch of road that was unbroken enough to allow them comfortable passage. Other times they found worn animal trails. Forests were the easiest walking of all. It was as if nature had come to terms with the forests long before. In fact, other than the occasional earthquake-produced scar in the earth, the forests seemed no different from the way they used to be before the apocalypse. At times they would come across large burned sections that had surrendered at some point in the past to lightning strikes and were now fostering new growth.

Progress continued to be slow, though. They always had to account for the new ravines that blocked their way. Sometimes they were tantalizingly narrow. Ben knew that if they didn't have Katie and Ralph with them, they could just jump.

One afternoon, they reached the crest of a hill and looked down to see a mile or more of narrow ravines stretched out ahead of them before ending at the edge of a forest. It was just beyond the convergence of numerous broken highways—now almost unseen from the plant growth. Ben looked to the right and the left. As far as the eye could see the ravines continued. He sat down heavily, unstrapping his backpack.

"Now what?" he asked.

Lila looked off to the left, then turned her head all the way to the right, having to compensate for the lack of vision on that side. "Either way we go, it's going to take us way out of our way. We don't even know how far the break-up continues. We can see right in front of us where we want to go. Can't be more than a mile. And some of the ravines are so narrow. It's like some great cosmic joke to drive us crazy. Unless...." She was looking down to the bottom of the hill her left. "Is that a Home Depot?"

"Looks like it might have been at one point," replied Ben.

"They sell—well, sold—ladders, right?" Ben nodded, knowing where this was going. "What if we find a solid, light-weight ladder to lay across the narrower cracks? Then we can just crawl across. When we're over, we can pull it across to use on the next one."

"You're a genius," said Ben. "I knew I kept you around for a reason." She smacked him on the arm. "And," he added, "if we find a couple of wooden or plastic shelves to lay along the ladder, it will make crossing a little easier.

Finding the ladders once they reached the store became a challenge. A good portion of the roof had collapsed, and the floor was all broken up, with plants growing high into the air. After a couple of hours of exploring, though, they ran across a twelve-foot aluminum ladder. Shelving was another matter. The best they could find was a thin and narrow four-foot piece of plywood. If nothing else, it would give them an illusion of the stability of a floor while they were climbing across the ladder.

It was late in the day, so they climbed back up the hill to a secluded spot among some rocks they had seen earlier. They set up camp and Ben went hunting with his crossbow while Lila and Katie, with Ralph, searched for vegetables.

Ben returned with two large rabbits. While Lila and Katie hadn't found any accessible vegetables, they came back with a bagful of late-season berries.

After they had eaten and put Katie to bed for the night, Ben and Lila settled down for what seemed like their first alone time in ages.

For a while, they just laid there listening to the sounds of the animals that had come alive for the night. As they snuggled closer, passion took over and they made love slowly and tenderly. Later, as they were drifting off, Lila rolled slightly to her right and Ben saw her fiddling with her eye patch. She lifted the patch up and rubbed under it, keeping her head turned away.

"That must be so uncomfortable," Ben said—a familiar refrain.

"It's not so bad." Lila's usual response.

"You should take it off at night. Give yourself a break from it."

"No, it's okay."

"Lila, don't you think I know the real reason? I know you're self-conscious about it, but there's no one around but us—and I'm the one who worked on it. Do you think I love you any less because of it? You will always be beautiful to me, with or without the patch. It hurts me that after all we've been through together, you would think something like that."

Lila rolled toward him and slowly lifted the patch off and set it aside.

It wasn't pretty, but neither was it ugly. The lid—which hadn't sustained damage—was mostly closed. The damaged eye had filmed over, but very little of it could be seen. But together with the comma-like scar under the eye, Ben could understand her self-consciousness. Her naturally shiny black hair and beautiful features were normally the first things that stood out, but now there was no getting past the eye.

And yet, she was far from ugly because of it. If anything, it made her look like a warrior, a battle-scarred beauty. Ben reached out and gently stroked the eye.

"This eye is part of who we are, what we've done, and where we've come from. If you want to wear the patch during the day, I understand, but don't hide it from me at night, okay?"

Lila leaned over and kissed him. "You're pretty amazing," she said, then frowned. "It must have been really hard for you for those months I retreated." Ben started to speak and Lila put her finger to his lips. "Don't say anything. I know it was. I'm sorry. It's hard to explain. After all the death I'd seen— including my parents—and all the people I'd killed. ... After all the viciousness I saw, the murders of all of those women and children in the camp by the lake, the months thinking you might be dead, it was this, of all things, that almost broke me. I'll never be able to explain to you—or maybe even to myself— exactly why, but it was. So thank you for staying with me and continuing to love me through it all. I know it's a cliché, but I came out of it a lot stronger."

Ben pulled her closer. "I know you did, babe" he mumbled, near sleep. "Maybe we both did."

Lila heard his soft breathing and kissed him softly on the cheek. "I love you," she whispered.

*****

They were up early the next morning, anxious to win the battle with the ravines.

"Why didn't we think of this before?" asked Ben, as they trudged down the hill wearing their backpacks and each carrying an end of the ladder. "How many miles did we waste trying to go around a crevasse that would have been accessible by laying a ladder across it?"

"Well, we have it now," answered Lila. "Hasn't that been the story of our whole existence for the last seven years? It's all been trial and error."

Their first crevasse was on the highway before the ravine field, and was only three feet wide and ten to fifteen feet deep—a good one to try out the ladder on. If something went wrong, they wouldn't fall into an unending abyss.

They laid the ladder across the crevasse and slid the piece of plywood out to the middle. The board was longer than the crevasse was wide.

"We don't take any chances," said Ben. "We always go across on hands and knees."

"And we tie a rope around Katie, with one of us always holding one end," added Lila. She knotted a twenty-foot length of rope under Katie's armpits, making sure it was snug.

"I can do it without the rope, mommy," objected Katie.

"I have no doubt that you can, sweetheart, but we have to be extra safe."

Ben was the first to go over. He could jump it, but that wasn't the purpose of this test. Besides, Katie would never be able to. She needed the ladder as a bridge. He started across, his backpack still on his back. Although the board was on the ladder, it was narrow and Ben had to crawl as much on the ladder rungs as the board. The rungs dug into his knees.

When he was across, Lila asked him how it had gone.

"Okay," he answered. "It's not comfortable, and I'm not sure the board isn't more of a nuisance than a help. Also, having the pack on my back was okay for this one, but if it's a wider crevasse, it might be more of a problem. It doesn't balance very well."

"So maybe we crawl across pushing our packs," suggested Lila. "Meanwhile, let's take off the board and see how Katie does with just the ladder."

Ben liked that suggestion and picked up the board and tossed it to the side. "Okay, Katie, your turn. Don't look down. This one isn't very deep, but some of the others will be and I want you to get into the habit of looking straight ahead."

He needn't have worried. She clambered across like a monkey, with Lila uselessly holding the rope. Next came Ralph, but the dog balked, reluctant to cross what he sensed was an unsafe situation. Ben realized that a dog would never be able to cross using the rungs of the ladder for support.

"Guess we need the board after all," he announced, and laid it back on the ladder. Ralph trotted across without a care. Lila followed, running into the same issues as Ben with the backpack.

They entered the large open field that contained the myriad cracks in the earth. The first couple were fairly simple, just a bit wider than the first one—although much deeper. But they knew that some of the crevasses in the middle of the field would present more of a challenge. The experiment of pushing the packs across ahead of them worked well.

An hour later they reached the middle of the field and a slightly wider crevasse. The fact that it took them an hour to go a half a mile pleased them to no end. Without the ladder as a bridge, they would probably still be looking for a place to cross the first crevasse.

This would be a tough one. It was close to ten feet across. Ben looked both ways up and down the ravine. Ten feet was about the best they were going to do. He and Lila laid the ladder across. Not much more than a foot of clearance on either side of the crevasse.

"I don't know if that's going to be enough support," he said. "The ladder might buckle in the middle."

"It's pretty sturdy," said Lila.

"So what you're saying is that I should give it a try," he said with a smirk. "You do know that my life insurance isn't paid up, right?"

"That's okay," replied Lila. "There are no banks to cash it in anyway."

A large pile of rocks sat by the edge of the crevasse. Ben picked up a medium-sized rock and placed it at the end of the ladder.

"This might help to keep it from sliding," he explained. "A couple more like that might do the trick."

"I'd feel better if we tied a rope around you, like we do with Katie," said Lila. "I can wrap it around a rock to secure it in case the ladder gives out."

"Okay," answered Ben. "What are we going to do about Ralph? The crevasse is about ten feet wide and the board is only four. He's not going to walk on the ladder without the board."

"I have an idea." Lila pulled down some rocks and leaned the board against them, securing it on both sides with more rocks, but leaving an empty space near one end. "Katie, would you like to use your crossbow and shoot a hole in the board?"

"Sure, mommy." They loaded her weapon while she prepared to shoot from a prone position. Once they handed her the crossbow, she aimed it like a pro and pulled the trigger. The bolt exploded through the wood, burying itself in the ground a few feet beyond the board.

Lila picked up the board. "Instant hole," she said. It was ragged and splintered from the force of the blow, but the board was still in one piece. "We can tie a rope to it and pull Ralph across. Great shooting, honey."

"Thanks, mommy. It was easy."

Once they determined that both the ladder and Ben were secure, Ben started slowly on his way across, pushing his pack ahead of him. While it didn't sag, Ben definitely felt more vulnerable on it than he had before.

He was a little more than halfway across when he picked up a familiar sound, one he hadn't heard in a long time. It was a motor—more than one. He looked off to his right. Traveling along the edge of the ravine were three trucks, and they were headed right for him!

Chapter 9

His mind quickly went back to the stories he had heard of the "evil," and how they used trucks to pick up innocent people. He made up his mind that there would be no way they would be taken.

Been there, done that, he thought. "Lila," he called out. "You and Katie hide behind the rocks and don't let them see you. I'll see if I can get back to you." But he knew that wouldn't happen. It was slow enough to try to push the pack forward on the unstable ladder, and it would be dangerous to attempt to turn around. No, he was stuck in the middle.

"Ben," Lila called back. "There is no way they are getting any of us. My rifle will be trained on them." Ben could hear her giving instructions to Katie.

Meanwhile, Ben wiggled backwards frantically, pulling his pack. But as the trucks approached, he realized that he was going to have to make his stand right there on the ladder. He looked down. He couldn't see the bottom. Only blackness. His position couldn't be any more precarious. He carefully unhooked his rifle from his pack and laid it across the ladder in front of him. Then he pulled out his pistol—the well-worn Sig Sauer 9mm that he had picked up the first day of their journey south so long ago—and wedged it into his pack where he could pull it free at a moment's notice.

The trucks pulled up. The first was an old Ford pick-up, the second a military-style truck with a canvas back—the type Ben had always seen in war movies. The third was unusual. It seemed to be a small tanker truck, but attached to the top was something that resembled a bridge. It was about twenty feet long and slightly wider than the truck it sat on. It looked to be made of a light metal. Aluminum?

Then it hit him. It was a bridge! It was the same idea as their ladder, but bigger. Big enough and strong enough to hold the trucks as they crossed over the crevasses. It was the only way trucks would be effective in this new churned-up world.

Two men stepped out of each vehicle and gathered around the end of the ladder. Only a couple of them carried rifles, but they all had holsters on their belts.

"What have we here?" asked one of them, staring over at Ben.

They were all wearing green military fatigues, but without any insignias or ranks sewn on, except the one who had spoken. He had blue fatigues and a bar of some sort on his shoulder, signifying his rank. Obviously the one in charge.

"You kind of look stuck. Need some help?"

"No thanks," answered Ben. "Doing just fine."

"Doesn't look like it to me," replied the man in blue. "In fact, this ladder looks pretty rickety. He bent down, grabbed the end, and gave it a little shake. "Definitely unsafe. You really shouldn't be on it." The other men were smirking, enjoying the show.

"I'll be fine, thanks."

"What are you doing way out here?"

"Just getting some air." Ben knew where this was going, so he had no reason to be cooperative.

"That your wife and kid behind the rocks?" He held up binoculars. "Yeah, we saw them from a long way off." He called out, "You can come out now."

There was no movement from behind the rocks.

"No reason to be afraid. We're not going to hurt you."

"Then what exactly are your intentions?" asked Ben.

"Kinda demanding for someone in such a vulnerable position."

"Just a question," said Ben. He had a good grip on his rifle and could bring it up and shoot in a second. His only worry was maintaining his balance on the ladder.

"Well then, I'll answer your question. We have a town. Getting to be a big one. We think you'd like it there. We'd like to invite you to come live there."

"Invite?"

"Yeah, well, you seem to be an intelligent guy. Maybe 'invite' is just one way to look at it. The other would be, we'd like to 'drag you, kicking and screaming.' That better? You kind of have your choice. For your family's sake, you might prefer the former."

"How about neither?"

"Not an option. Listen," he softened a little—an obvious ploy to give Ben an out. "Life sucks out here. It's no kind of life for your little girl. Do you remember the world before all this?

Do you remember the comfort of electricity? Well, we have it. The whole town is powered by electricity. So it's really for your own good that you come."

"I think I can judge that for myself. So now I'll give you your options. You guys can get into your trucks and drive away, or you can be cut down where you stand." He lifted his rifle and pointed it at them, setting it on top of his pack for support. "And you'll be first."

The man took a slight step back, all the while, trying to maintain an air of superiority.

"You shoot me and you'll be dead in a second."

"Maybe, maybe not. Regardless, you'll be dead."

The two men with rifles raised them simultaneously. As if in slow motion, Ben saw the leader bring up his hands, as if to tell his men not to shoot. Ben heard the loud boom from behind the rocks, and saw one of the men propelled backwards, his rifle flying. A moment later, Ben fired—not at the leader, but at the other rifleman. His shot went high, taking off the top of the man's head. He crumpled to the ground. Ben's ears were ringing. His shot had echoed off the walls of the crevasse below him.

The leader threw up his hands, with the remaining three following suit.

"Okay, you made your point," he said. "We'll drive away."

"No you won't," said Ben. "You lost that chance. We'll let you go, but not with your trucks. You're not going to do to anyone else what you tried to do to us. Undo your holsters and drop them to the ground, then move away from the trucks and lie on your stomachs with your hands on your heads."

The men did as he asked, and Ben began his crawl along

the ladder toward them.

"I've got them covered," Lila called out.

Ben addressed the men, who were now all in a prone position. "She's always been a better shot than me, so I really suggest you don't move."

I killed my first man—three, to be exact—the day Lila was almost raped on our journey down from Massachusetts. Under the circumstances, it was surprisingly easy to do, as were the ones that followed. But we both reached the point where it began to sicken us. So when we found our cabin by the lake, we thought it was all behind us. Then, when we started on our way to Yellowstone, we were hoping that the chaos that had dominated the country the months after the event would have now been replaced by, well, if not a sense of normalcy, then at least some cooperation or common sense. It was depressing to find that some things hadn't, in fact, changed at all.

Ben reached the other side and scrambled to his feet. He picked up the men's holsters and threw them into the crevasse. Meanwhile, Lila had come out from behind the rocks and stood near the edge of the crack with her rifle trained on the group. Katie was by her side, looking a little confused, but not scared. Ralph was right by Katie's side, instinctively knowing that things weren't quite right and that his job was to guard Katie.

"So here's what you are going to do," Ben informed them. "You will take the little bridge you have on top of the tanker truck and put it over the crevasse."

"We need all six of us for that."

"You have four of you. Make it work."

"It's heavy."

"Doesn't look that heavy."

"Trust me, it is."

"Not my problem. I suggest you get started. And I really hope you don't try anything or there will only be three of you. It'll be even heavier."

They got to it. It was clear that with all six, they had it down to a science and could get it down in a matter of minutes. It was a combination of pulleys and sheer strength. Two fewer people threw off the whole routine and it took them almost an hour to move the bridge into position over the crevasse. They were exhausted by the end of it and were happy when Ben told them to sit. Lila, Katie, and Ralph used the bridge and crossed the gorge with ease.

"Here's how this is going to work," said Ben. "You will put your vehicles in neutral and push them into the gorge."

"But then we will have to walk," said one of them.

A mental genius, thought Ben. "No shit, Sherlock. Just like all the rest of us. And after you push them in the gorge, you will do exactly that, you will start walking … away from us. I don't care where you go. You're not going to be able to cross the ravines, so I suggest walking parallel to one of them. Eventually you will find places to cross." He looked at the leader. "That's your only choice, and it's not an invitation."

One by one, the trucks were pushed into the gorge. The pick-up fell to the bottom with a tremendous crash. A minute later, a cloud of dust surfaced and rose into the air. The other two trucks made it part-way down before getting stuck. It didn't matter to Ben. They were stuck for good.

"You can go," announced Ben.

An hour later, Ben, Lila, Katie, and Ralph had crossed four more narrow crevasses using the ladder, and were safely in the forest on the other side.

The four men were dots on the horizon.

Chapter 10

The ladder continued to work well for them over the next couple of days. It wasn't heavy, but it was awkward, and at times they resented having the cumbersome load. But they couldn't complain about its effectiveness. They still had to skirt around many of the wider ravines, which was time-consuming, but unavoidable.

On the third day after their encounter with the men in the trucks, Ben made a decision that almost proved catastrophic. They were once again faced with a wide ravine—narrow enough for the ladder to fit across, but wide enough that it made the crossing stressful. The ravine continued as far as they could see in either direction.

"Cross?" asked Ben.

"One scary and potentially dangerous hour versus maybe a day or two of walking to find the end of the ravine or an easier place to cross."

"If anything," said Ben, "it looks like it actually gets wider in both directions. I say we should try it."

"You haven't steered us wrong yet."

There was always a first time.

Ben tied a rope to the ladder just in case, then slowly slid it out across the crevasse. When it became too front-heavy, he gave it an extra push to reach the other side. It just barely made it. He pushed it a little further, until there was about a foot and a half of ladder on each side of the seemingly bottomless pit. It was about the same margin he had on the ravine he was crossing when they encountered the men.

"I'm not going to push my backpack across," he said to Lila. "I think I'll go across, then throw you the rope. You can tie it to my pack and I'll pull it over the ladder. I'll bring the other packs the same way, then Katie, then you. That work?"

"It works for me as long as you tie yourself to the rope when you go over. There's a good tree to wrap the rope around, and then I'll hold it, like before."

The details taken care of, Ben tied the rope to his ankle and started across. Lila wrapped the rope twice around the tree and slowly let out the tension as Ben crawled. Katie and Ralph sat off to the side and watched.

Although the crevasse was no wider than the first one, Ben found himself more nervous.

"Piece of cake," he told himself, not believing a word of it. By the time he reached the halfway point, he knew it was a mistake. He didn't want Lila or Katie attempting it. He was also sure that Ralph would balk at it. Was it the depth? He couldn't see the bottom the last time either, but this felt deeper. He stopped.

"Coming back," he called out.

"You okay?" called out Lila.

"Doesn't feel right."

"Okay. Come back slowly. Be careful."

"I will." He felt the ladder move and he looked to the other side. The ledge wasn't stable and the edge was crumbling. "Hold the ro…" he started to call out. The ladder broke free. The last thing he heard as he descended into the abyss was Lila's scream. He fell about twenty feet until the rope stopped him suddenly and painfully. He hit the side wall of the crevasse hard and everything went black.

*****

"Oh no … oh no … oh no," Lila cried out in a panicked voice. She heard Katie scream. The tension on the rope was tight, so she knew Ben was still there. That part was good, but she could feel the rope slipping. Even though she had wrapped it twice around the tree, it wasn't enough. Ben's weight was more than it could bear.

"Katie, honey. Call out to daddy. See if he's okay. Don't go too near the side."

"Okay." Katie assumed a half-scared/half-serious expression and stopped ten feet from the pitch. "Daddy!" she cried out. No answer. She tried it again. Ralph got into the act and started barking. "Quiet, Ralph. I can't hear if daddy is calling." Ralph went silent. Katie called out again, but heard nothing in response.

"Mommy, I can't hear daddy." There was a quaver in her voice.

"Keep trying honey. And keep listening."

Lila was losing her battle with the rope. If she could somehow loop her end around the rope leading from Ben to the tree, she could buy herself some time and maybe get a strong knot in it, but she had to hurry. She had about five feet to play with, but in another minute she'd only have a fraction of that and her window of opportunity would be gone. Katie! Katie could help.

"Honey, I need you ... quickly." Katie abandoned her vigil at the crevasse and ran over. Already Lila had lost another foot. "Take this end of the rope and loop it over that other part of the rope."

"The straight one?"

"Yes, honey, the straight one."

Katie took the end from Lila and dropped it over the top of the rope that led from the tree to Ben.

"Okay, now pull it through and bring it back to me."

When Katie handed it to her, she pulled and the slipping stopped. Not done yet, she tied a knot and slowly let go of the rope, hoping the knot would hold. It did. She sank to the ground to catch her breath, but only for a moment. When she stopped shaking, she quickly got up and said to Katie, "I need you to stay here and keep an eye on the rope. See that knot?" Katie nodded. "If you see it move at all, you let me know, okay?"

"Okay, mommy. Is daddy going to be okay?"

"I'm sure he will. I have to go try to help him up. You've been an awesome help."

She ran to the side and peered down. Once her eye got used to the gloom, she could make out the bottom of Ben's boot. He was still upside down. "Ben, can you hear me?"

Nothing.

"Ben, you've got to wake up." Her voice echoed back to her.

She tried pulling on the rope, but Ben's dead weight made it impossible to lift him. She sat down with tears in her eyes. She needed him to wake up. There was no way to bring him to the surface otherwise. Suddenly, she had an idea. After checking again with Katie that the knot was secure, she ran to her backpack and grabbed her flashlight, her canteen, and a second bottle of water and went back to the ledge. She shone the light. He definitely wasn't moving. Even with the flashlight, it was difficult to see his head, but she thought she saw a blood patch. If that was the case, he might be losing blood quickly, and time was of the essence. She opened the bottle of water and very slowly poured it down the hole, hoping to catch Ben's head. It was hard to line it up at first, but finally she could see it hit it's mark.

If this didn't wake him, she wasn't sure anything would.

*****

It was raining. It was nighttime and Ben was caught without shelter. But where were Lila and Katie? The rain was only a trickle at the moment running down his face and dripping off his head, but he knew how quickly the storms could intensify. Wait. Dripping down off the top of his head? That didn't make sense. And his head was killing him. What happened? Slowly it began to dawn on him. He seemed to be hanging in midair. Panic set in. He thrashed about, trying to grab hold of something solid. He could feel the rope around his ankle. It was painful. He touched something cold and smooth. Rock. A rock wall.

And then it all came back. The ladder falling and him hitting something hard. The rain stopped and he heard a voice calling his name. It was Lila!

"Ben, wake up."

He groaned in response. He felt his head and realized he'd been bleeding. A lot. A scary amount.

"Are you okay?"

He found his voice. "The ladder fell. I hit something."

"I can't lift you. Can you climb out?"

"The rock wall is smooth. I'll feel around." He was beginning to get his wits back.

"Hurry! I knotted the other end around the tree, but I just don't trust it."

"And I think the knot around my ankle is beginning to slip." That was an understatement. He was trying not to worry Lila. In fact, the rope had slipped a lot. He changed the angle of his foot to keep the rope from sliding off, but that was only going to be a very temporary measure. He had to take the pressure off the rope somehow. He felt around. There was nothing to grab on to.

Where are the trees and roots like the ones growing out of all the other crevasses? He thought. He felt along the wall for something … anything … to grab. It wasn't working, and now the rope was dangerously close to slipping off his foot. He abandoned his search for a foothold and focused his attention on the rope.

He was weak from the fall and dizzy from the loss of blood. He needed to grab hold of the rope, but it meant doing a sit-up from his upside down, dead-weight position and reaching the rope around his ankle—not easy in the best of circumstances. If he could hold onto something on the wall, it would help.

A crack! Not big, but enough to fit his fingers into. He wedged them in and tried to pull himself up. Nothing. He was weaker than he thought.

"Lila," he called. "I have a bad situation here. The rope is coming off my foot, but I can't reach it. I need help. You don't have to pull me all the way up, but just give me something to help me bend at the waist so I can reach the rope. Do we have anything? Anything at all?"

"Let me look."

"Look fast! Please."

*****

Lila jumped up and ran to the backpacks. She tore through them, finding nothing. She looked around. There had to be something that could help. She looked at Katie, who was still monitoring the knot.

"It's still on the tree, mommy."

"That's good, honey," she said distractedly. And then it hit her. The tree! There was a low branch right above Katie's head. It wasn't too thick—she thought she might be able to break it off.

"Katie, move out of the way, please."

As Katie moved, Lila jumped at the branch and pulled it down. It bent but it didn't break. She pulled again and again. Finally, she could feel it begin to splinter. A minute later it snapped off. She dragged it to the edge of the ravine. She didn't even know if it was long enough.

"Ben?"

"Still here ... for the moment, anyway."

"I have a branch. I hope it can reach you. I can't pull you up though."

"Don't need you to. I just need something to give me a little support." Ben had his foot turned at an unnatural angle to keep the knot on. "Let's try it."

Lila leaned over the side of the crevasse and dangled the branch as far as she could. Ben could see the thin end—would it break off if he grabbed it?—but he couldn't quite reach it.

"So close. Can you get it any closer?"

"No. It's as far as I can go and still keep my grip." There was panic in her voice.

"Okay then. Hold on to it tight. It might jerk when I grab it." If I can grab it, he thought.

Lila had a knob at the end that she wrapped her fingers around for support.

"Okay. I'm ready."

Ben knew he'd have one chance, and one chance only. He had to summon the strength to bend up even just a few inches. But if he couldn't, it would be all over. He would never have the strength to try it twice.

"Here goes." He screamed at the top of his lungs to release as much energy as possible and bent at the waist and jerked himself up. It wasn't much. Only a few inches. But it was enough to grab the branch.

Lila felt the jerk—even stronger than she was prepared for—and almost lost the branch, but she managed to keep her grip. If she hadn't had the knob for support, the whole branch would have slipped from her hands.

Now that he had a little leverage, Ben lifted himself up until he touched the rope. With one last push, he grabbed the rope with both hands. His foot slipped from the knot, and all of a sudden he was hanging from the rope by his hands. The situation wasn't much better, as his strength was fading. He brought up his leg and tried to find the loop the knot made. He put his foot in the loop and used it as a step, standing himself upright. He wasn't worried about the loop and the knot. The knot was secure. It had just been tied too loosely on his ankle.

"Are you okay?" Lila called out.

"I am. Just resting." He had a clear view of Lila now. He felt he could almost touch her, but she was still about ten feet above him. He could also see the sides of the crevasse clearly now. Nearer the top the sides were not as smooth, and the roots were plentiful. He rested a minute longer, then very carefully, while still maintaining a good grip on the rope, he began to make the climb.

The roots were sturdy and in a matter of minutes he was within arm's reach of Lila. She grabbed his hand and pulled. A minute later he was lying on the grass at the top of the crevasse taking in great gasps of air. Lila was cleaning his head wound. As with many cuts to the head, he had lost a fair amount of blood, but the wound wasn't serious. Katie ran over and, as a family, they hugged, with Ben and Lila telling Katie how brave she had been.

They camped that night under the tree, any thought of finding a replacement ladder totally dismissed. The irony of the situation was that the next morning they found a crossing point less than a mile from the spot of Ben's fall.

Even in our old world, life was fragile. The simplest mistake could end in serious injury or death. In the new world, those chances were increased exponentially. On one hand we were more aware, but on the other hand, danger lurked almost everywhere. I was lucky ... this time. I wondered though, was it going to be some fluke event like that one that would eventually kill me?

Chapter 11

They walked for two weeks without seeing another person. Once they saw smoke coming from a chimney a couple miles away, but decided not to make contact. They were making good time, but Ben always made sure they took numerous breaks and quit for the day by mid-afternoon. While Katie was used to playing in the woods and had boundless energy and endurance, she was still only six and couldn't go on forever. In Lila's case, Ben called it quits when she would start to limp noticeably. Lila never complained about the early end to their day and seemed willing to let Ben call the shots. And of course, he was fine about stopping early in deference to his own condition. His injuries weren't serious, but were painful and became more so after hours of walking.

They stayed away from the remains of towns as much as possible, but avoiding them altogether was out of the question. Like the earlier towns they had encountered, most were overgrown and many had also been ravaged by fire. Between the fires immediately after the event caused mostly from people dying with lit cigarettes, fires caused by the earthquakes, and those started by lightning, it was hard to find a town that had remained fairly intact. It was even rarer to find one untouched, not overgrown, and populated. Which was why when they finally walked into one, it was a complete surprise.

The hand-painted sign read: Monett, Mo.

When they passed the sign, they thought they had gone back in time—to two very different eras. The first was the time before the event—mowed lawns, houses that had been taken care of, clean concrete streets, and people talking and laughing. And the people were clean, with clean clothes. But the second era was almost as prevalent in the scene. It dated back to the 1800s. There were no cars, no motorcycles, no gas lawnmowers. Light posts had been taken down, as had street lights and power lines. Transportation was by bicycle or by horse.

They entered the town a little after noon, Ben figured, judging by the sky. The first people they encountered were three women talking together in the street. Three children younger than Katie were playing with a ball. The only thing odd about the scene was the fact that each woman had a handgun in a holster attached to her belt.

The women came as a group to greet the travelers. Ben was sure that the presence of Katie put them at ease.

"Welcome to Monett," said the first. She was probably in her late-thirties, thought Ben. She was pretty, but had the lines in her face of someone who had suffered mightily at some point in the past. Ben wasn't sure they'd ever meet anyone who didn't have those lines.

"Thank you," said Lila. "This," she said, sweeping her hand around, "is quite a surprise. What a beautiful community."

"Well, we've tried. My name is Sharon, and this is Antoinette and Belinda," she said, pointing to the other two women. "And the children running around are Connor, Corey, and Janette."

"I'm Lila, and this is my husband Ben, our daughter Katie, and Ralph the dog."

Ben could tell that the names Ben and Lila meant something to her. Not in a positive or negative way, but more surprised than anything else.

"You have to meet our mayor," said Sharon. "He should be in his office. Follow me."

"When did you start the town?" asked Ben as they were walking.

"Four years ago. There were two groups of us—about seventy altogether—who met about a hundred miles east of here. Both groups had been living in makeshift camps and were tired of it. We combined forces and were determined to find a town to call our own. As you know, most towns were destroyed by one thing or another, but we knew we'd find something. When we walked into Monett, we knew we had arrived. Most of the town was in ruins, but there was one section that had escaped the devastation. It's only a few blocks wide and long, but it's plenty big enough for us. Over time, more people drifted in, and of course babies were born, so our population is up to 165." She stopped in front of what was once a private home. Now it had a sign that read: Monett Town Office. "Follow me."

She opened the front door and called out, "Brian, we have guests."

A nice-looking man in his early thirties came out of an office, stopped, and smiled. "You're still not going to kill me, right?" he asked, looking at Ben.

"Oh my God," said Ben, and went over and gave the man a hug. He turned to Lila. "Lila, you don't know Brian, but I met him twice when I was separated from you. The last time I saw him, he saved my life as I was leaving Washington."

"That's okay, you more than saved my life by letting me go after you killed my 'colleagues'," he said, making quotation marks in the air. Then he turned serious. "Actually, I do know Lila, and I don't know if it's too late to apologize."

"Oh, right," said Ben. "Of course. You were one of the guards at the camp where Lila was being held."

"It's not too late to apologize," said Lila, stepping forward. "Frankly, I never saw you as one of them. You seemed different. You weren't cruel in any way. You seemed lost, if anything."

"I was lost. In many ways, your husband freed me. I've worked hard to try to erase that time of my life. We have a real community here, and I'm so happy to be a part of it. Are you here to stay?"

"No," said Ben. "Just passing through."

"Doesn't surprise me. At least stay for a few days. We've set up some guest quarters. You can stow your gear, then I can show you around."

As they walked out of the office, Brian said, "I knew you were living by the lake, but really didn't know if you were still alive after all this time. Most people think you're dead."

That statement was getting old. There was nothing they could say.

"Even after all this time, your names still carry great weight."

"This is a long way from there," said Lila. "Hard to believe people have heard of us."

"Let me guess," said Brian. "You've been by the lake and out of touch until just recently?"

"Forest fire," replied Ben. "A few weeks ago. Until then we hadn't seen anyone in a few years."

"Well, there's a lot you need to catch up on. In general, people have been migrating west. A lot of that was due to the plague. You've heard about it?"

"We have."

As they walked, Ben and Lila marveled at the town of Monett. They could sense the destruction beyond the new community's borders, but none of that permeated the comfort that surrounded them. In most cases, existing homes had been taken over by individual families, but numerous new structures had gone up as well. Every house had a large garden, now done for the year, and stacks of wood. They passed several people, all of whom seemed content. An old church had survived and now doubled as a school. Brian pointed it out as they walked by.

"We have about 125 adults and 40 children living here. The school run like an old two-room schoolhouse. We have two teachers—one for the older kids and one for the younger ones."

"Any electricity?" asked Ben.

"No. Frankly, I'm not so sure people miss it all that much. They are just so happy to be living a somewhat normal life again. Maybe someday, but in all honesty, I doubt it."

"You were going to tell us about the plague," said Lila.

"We heard a little bit about it."

"It was massive. Considering how few people were left in this country, it was the last thing we needed. It affected the whole east coast, from what I hear. We were already here when it hit. We got the full report from refugees." His face darkened. "We took in a few who seemed plague-free and were willing to be quarantined for a month in houses outside the town. Others, we had to send away. That was hard. We even had to shoot two people who tried to force themselves into the town. It was a tough time for us."

"It was the whole east coast?" asked Ben.

"As far as we know. The major cities were largely abandoned, but a lot of smaller settlements had sprung up on the outskirts. The plague ravaged them."

"We heard DC was gone," said Ben. "I assume that means President Jeffries, too?"

"From what I hear. It's too bad. I liked the man. He was really trying to put things back together. Don't know how successful he would have been, but he was trying."

"I had two friends there. Dan and Gordon. Did you know them?"

"I did. They talked a lot about you two. Dan might still be alive. He left Washington before me. Just didn't take to the city. I think Gordon's death bothered him, too. Just needed some new surroundings. I know he was headed west, but I have no idea where. I don't think he did either."

"How did Gordon die?"

"Suicide. He was never the same after his wife was killed. Went into an abandoned building and shot himself."

They were quiet for a minute, then Lila said, "So whoever

was left in the east headed west?"

"For the most part. I'd guess that there are very few people between Florida and Massachusetts."

Ben thought about Rob, Jenny, and Amber. It could be that the community they were heading for no longer existed.

They reached the guest quarters, a small house at the edge of town.

"It's not much, but it does the job," said Brian. "There are three bedrooms, but if you could all sleep in one, it leaves the other two open in case any others arrive."

"Do you get many?" asked Lila.

"A few, here and there. When they do come through, it's usually in groups of five to ten, so they take the whole house. Anyway, I'll give you time to freshen up. You can take a shower. We've put cisterns on top of all the houses. They catch the rainwater—we get plenty of that with all the storms. We've set up showers and baths in the houses. Your woodstove isn't going, so I would suggest a shower for now. Won't be warm, but it's something. Later, you can start the stove if you'd like, and warm up water for a bath. When you feel refreshed, come on back to the office and we can talk more."

"Thank you, Brian, for all the hospitality," said Ben.

"You'd do the same. In fact, when I originally headed west, I was going to take you up on your invitation and stop by your house on the lake, but the damn crevasses kept me headed in the wrong direction. Finally, I gave up. Oh," he added. "Feel free to leave your rifles and crossbows here when you do come back. You won't need them. I do suggest keeping your pistols on you, though."

Ben raised his eyebrows.

"Long story. One for another time."

Monett was the first sign of normalcy we had found since the event. People didn't look scared. They didn't look exhausted. They seemed happy, comfortable, and, well, normal. But below the surface there must have been something, something that required them to wear their weapons. And I had no doubt we'd find out what that was in due time.

Chapter 12

It was wonderful to relax and rid themselves of their heavy belongings. They all took showers. The water was cold, but bearable. Lila put Katie down for a nap—a habit they had gotten into living by the lake.

"You look tired, too," said Ben.

"I think I need to rest my eye. I feel like it's doing double-duty."

"That's because it is."

"You look raring to go," said Lila. "Why don't you go meet with Brian while I rest. We can meet up later."

"Okay. That sounds good." He went over to her and gave her a hug and a long, slow kiss. "I love you so much," he said.

"And I love you. We've been through so much and have had to endure major changes, but the one thing that has never changed is my love for you."

They just stood there hugging, until Lila playfully pushed him away. "Get out. Go see the town and report back. I'll keep Ralph here. He probably needs the rest, too."

Ben saluted and was out the door.

It felt odd to be without his backpack, rifle, and crossbow. He instinctively touched the pistol at his side.

Whether word had gotten around about Ben and Lila and people were curious, or whether they were just particularly welcoming to newcomers, it seemed to Ben that everyone in town made a point of shaking hands with him and introducing themselves. Either way, it was sincere. He decided to walk around and get the lay of the land before going to see Brian.

They had picked well. The town consisted of an area of about five city blocks built on the edge of a former golf course. How the earthquake had spared that one section was a mystery. And yet, they had come across similar large areas of untouched land. This was the first one this large that he had seen in a town. They had put up a chain-link fence around the edges of the town, not to keep the people in, but to physically separate the new town from its former incarnation.

Near the center of town was what Ben could only call a slaughtering station. A deer hung from hooks, as did a couple of wild turkeys and numerous rabbits.

"It's where people come to clean their kills," said a man who had come up quietly behind Ben. He was older, probably in his sixties, wearing a baseball cap with very little under it. He put out his hand. "Walt."

He shook his hand. "Ben."

"Welcome to Monett."

"Thanks. What do they do with the meat?"

"Pass it out. Anyone who is in need of meat for dinner can pick it up here."

"No charge of any kind?"

"Nope. Everyone here contributes in some way. If you are skilled at carpentry, you offer your services to anyone who needs it. Same is true of just about everything else. We have no money. I guess you could call it bartering, but it's not like anyone keeps track. If you need something done and there is someone who can do it, they do."

"So different from our old world."

"Some people have said it's true Socialism or Communism, or maybe even Democracy at its best, but it's not really. There is no label. It's just appreciation. We've all come through a lot. I don't know your story—although there are rumors floating around—but when all is said and done, I'm sure it's not all that different from anyone else's. We've all suffered. We've all managed to find the strength to keep on going when so many couldn't. And now we've come together. Would it make sense to revert back to our old life? Isn't that what got us into this mess to begin with? Greed, anger, selfishness? We have no use for it. We decided from the very beginning that we would run this town differently. It's not to say that we don't have arguments from time to time, but they're minor. No, this is working and people seem content with it."

They were joined by Brian.

"Saw you over here, and figured I'd save you the walk to my office."

"Walt was just explaining the philosophy here. Impressive."

"Some of the early residents said it wouldn't work. When it started to be successful, they just naturally moved on. The people here are the ones who want to be here." He looked around. "Where's Lila?"

"Sleeping," said Ben. "The rest will do her good."

"What happened to her eye, if that's not too personal."

"Bar fight. You should see the other guy."

Brian and Walt stared at him for a minute, then Brian smiled. "Had me for a minute."

So Ben told them the story, as well as the details about her ankle.

"We do have a doctor in town, though I doubt he'd be much good to Lila at this point. Have a veterinarian, too. I told you about the two teachers. We don't have a priest or minister for the church, but it's kind of worked out for the best. Those who want to can take turns leading the services. We try to keep on spiritual topics. Everyone seems to like it."

Walt excused himself, explaining that he had to go fix a shower.

"So what are your plans?" asked Brian.

"We heard there was a settlement at Yellowstone. We were thinking of trying it out. Do you know anything about it?"

"I do. We had a few people come through here who had been there. Very different from here."

"How so?"

"We're a closer community. Physically closer—like a regular town. From what I'm told, the Yellowstone settlement is a lot larger, but really spread out. They have a town center, but the houses are spread out in the hills."

"It's kind of what we are looking for—a strong community, but with the privacy we've been used to."

"Was kinda hoping you'd stay here."

"Well, I haven't talked to Lila, so we will definitely keep it under consideration. Tell me about the guns."

"Yes, the guns." Brian frowned. "Let's walk."

It was a beautiful sunny day, but as was often the case in their new world, a black sky was just on the horizon. In an hour or two it would be pouring.

"The main reason—or, the initial reason, I should say—that we asked everyone to be armed was for protection from animal attacks. Believe it or not, when this group first got together four years ago, there were still people who hadn't handled a gun, and had no desire to. I had to wonder how they had survived so long. We tried to establish our community with as few rules as possible, but one rule a number of us insisted on was that every able-bodied adult carry a weapon and know how to use it. We spent a lot of time teaching them. And it worked. Every adult in Monett carries a handgun and is fairly skilled at its use. Some of the older children, too. Katie is young, but my guess is that you've already taught her the basics."

"Not with guns, yet," answered Ben. "But with the smaller crossbow, she's a dead shot."

"Well, it paid off for us. We had a lot of attacks by dog packs, and people were prepared. The dogs pretty well steer clear of us now. Having the fence around much of the town helps, too."

"You said that was the initial reason," said Ben. "Does the other reason have something to do with the evil?"

"I've heard it called that. We refer to it as 'Nebraska,' because that's where they are from."

"I think we ran into some of them about two weeks back."

Brian's faced sagged. "You saw them east of here? That means they're back. Tell me about them."

So Ben gave him a complete rundown of the encounter.

"That was one of their smaller outfits," explained Brian. "If you know anything about them at all, you've probably heard that they are trying to 'collect' people. A smaller outfit like that would be good for individuals and small groups that they might run across, like your family. The larger outfits supposedly have double the trucks and men. They are systematically going from settlement to settlement and rounding up the people."

"And you're worried that they will be here soon."

"They already have been. A small group like the one you encountered. They came by earlier this year. I think they were just feeling us out. They acted all friendly-like, but it was clear that they were anything but. They wanted to let us know about their town. They were really pushing the fact that they had power. They didn't fool anyone though. We had already heard the rumors, so we sent them on their way. I'm worried about one of the bigger groups, though. With 125 adults, we could defend ourselves pretty well, and probably drive them away. But we always need to be armed and ready. If they catch us off-guard, we're in trouble. You probably didn't notice," he said, pointing to the far corner of the settlement, "but we have a tower over there. There is always someone manning it. They look for dog packs, marauders, and most importantly, Nebraska."

"What do you know about Nebraska?" asked Ben.

"Probably not a whole lot more than you do. Whoever, or whatever group's behind it has a plan that they seem to be carrying out with precision. They have electricity and vehicles. I have to assume that they are trying to rebuild some sort of society, but not with the best of intentions, as you've already experienced."

Brian stopped and looked around carefully before continuing. "Here's my fear. Based on the stories I hear, they are pretty unstoppable, and if that's the case, we don't stand a chance. Sure, maybe we repel the first group, and even the second. Eventually though, they'll just come at us with too big of a force. And then what? Once they've taken over much of the country, are we going to be in any better shape than we were right after the apocalypse? The despair will be just as bad. There'll be no freedoms. We might as well have just perished when everyone else did. The east coast had its plague. Now we have our own plague. And I don't know if we can stop it."

Something was being left unsaid, and I knew it. The downside to having a reputation was that everyone expected you to live up to it. Brian was asking for our help. But help with what? Fighting the Nebraska raiders? Brian knew it was just a temporary fix. Eventually Nebraska would win. It seemed to be a lose-lose situation. And yet....

There was nothing more to say. From Brian's standpoint, he had put the bug in Ben's ear. There was nothing more he could do. For Ben's part, it was time to talk to Lila.

As he walked into the house, he was greeted with the aroma of roast turkey and freshly-baked bread. Lila had the table set, and she and Katie were sitting, waiting for Ben. Both had brushed their hair, and put on clean clothes. Katie looked like a miniature version of Lila, with her long, black hair. Both were smiling.

"I saw you coming," said Lila, "so we put out the food. Thought you might like to eat at a table for a change."

"We made all this, daddy," Katie said with a grin. "Just kidding!"

Ben was speechless. "Where did it come from?" he finally said.

"Sharon and the other two women we met brought it all over a few minutes ago. I can't believe it. It's more than we can eat. I asked if they wanted to join us, but they said we needed some down time after all of our walking."

Ben washed his hands and sat down. "This is amazing," he said, biting into a slice of wild turkey."

"How was your time with Brian?" asked Lila.

"Interesting. I'll tell you later."

"Good interesting or bad interesting?"

"Not sure. The jury is still out."

*****

Later, as he was putting Katie down for the night, she looked up at him and said, "Daddy, I like this place. Can we stay?"

"I don't know, honey. We'll see."

"Well I hope so," she said, as she drifted off to sleep, with Ralph sleeping at the end of the bed.

When Ben got back to the living room, Lila said, "I heard what Katie said. I think she's tired of walking."

"I don't blame her. I think we all are."

He proceeded to tell her about his talk with Brian, and his spoken request that they stay, and unspoken request for help.

"Your thoughts?" asked Ben.

"I haven't seen much of the town yet, but it seems pleasant. This house is certainly comfortable, but …"

"It's not us," finished Ben.

"Exactly. There's a reason Yellowstone appeals to us, and maybe we've been spoiled. We had the perfect situation near the lake—except for the socialization for Katie. It just seems like we belong there."

"How about this as a solution?" asked Ben. "We knew starting out that we'd never reach Yellowstone by winter. And even if we did, I assume we'd have to build a cabin, which takes time. Why don't we stay here for the winter and leave in the spring. Then we could get to Yellowstone in time to get set up."

"That sounds good to me. What are we going to do about Brian's veiled request for help?"

What we always did.

Chapter 13

The next day was busy. Ben informed Brian that they would stay for the fall and winter, and into the spring, but couldn't guarantee anything beyond that. Brian accepted that with pleasure and, Ben noticed, a fair amount of relief.

"But I need to know," said Ben after discussing their plans with Brian, "how you are going to need us to help. It's obvious that you want help with the Nebraska threat."

"Am I that transparent?" asked Brian.

"Kind of."

"The truth is, I have no idea if we will see them this fall. As I said before, we are a pretty big settlement, and it would take a lot of planning on their part to take us. But regardless of that, some preparation on our part is necessary. Whether they come this fall or next year, we have to be ready. We don't really have anyone here capable of doing that kind of battle planning. Don't get me wrong. Everyone here is willing to do their part. They've survived all this time, and they had to develop a good amount of toughness to do that. But they are not soldiers. Hell,

I'm not either, for that matter. I was kind of thrown into this role by chance. They are all ready to fight if they need to. They just need someone to lead them."

"And you think that person is me? Or me and Lila?" Brian nodded. Ben looked at the ground, a feeling growing in his gut. He couldn't tell if it was dread, or whether he could detect a little excitement there. He looked up. "I'm not a battlefield general. Lila may look the part of a warrior, but she really isn't. We are just two people who did what we had to do to survive. No different from anyone here."

"Very different from everyone here," corrected Brian. "I don't think you quite realize your skills. I heard the stories…" Ben started to object, but Brian cut him off. "…and I know many of them were exaggerated. But give me some credit for knowing the difference. The thing is, you were both clear-headed when it came to battle. You didn't just show courage, you used your brains. You strategized. We need that trait here. A lot of our people are ready to confront attackers with guns blazing, but that's not necessarily what we need." He took a breath. "Just help us develop a plan. That's all I ask."

Ben knew there was no way he could say no. He nodded and they shook hands. At that moment, Lila, Katie, and Ralph joined them.

"I have a house for you," Brian said, now that the important discussion was done. "We still have a half a block of unoccupied houses down in the lower part of the town. They all need a little work, but you can take your pick. They've been fitted for running water from cisterns on the roof, wood stoves, and the chimneys are clean. Let me show you."

As they walked, a pair of horses with riders passed them.

Lila stopped, bringing the others to a halt, as well. "It just hit me," she said. "We've seen horses here, but no stable. Where do you keep them?"

Leave it to Lila to notice that, thought Ben.

"Ah, yes," replied Brian. "We haven't told you about the farms. About a mile down the road from here is our horse stable—or stables, I should say. It's big. We have close to 200 horses there. Further up the road is a farm, and still further is a ranch. Over the years we've rounded up cattle, pigs, chickens, sheep, goats, and horses. We have close to 600 head of cattle— lots of milk cows and lots of cattle for food. Needless to say, we have plenty of milk—we make our own butter, too—and plenty of eggs from the chickens. We still try to hunt much of our food, but when times get a bit leaner, like in the winter, we never go hungry. Everyone here has his own horse, including most of the children—even many of the younger ones. We'll show you the ones that haven't already been taken and the three of you can choose your own."

Ben and Lila glanced at each other, and Brian caught the meaning.

"Let me guess," he said. "You've never ridden before." They shook their heads. "No problem," he assured them. "Many of the people here, including me, had never ridden before. We have a couple of really good horse people. They can help you find the right ones and teach you how to ride. If you end up leaving in the spring, you can take them with you—our gift to you. They'll make your trip to Yellowstone a lot easier. Even if you have to go many miles out of your way to get over a crevasse, you won't mind so much, because you won't be doing the work. So let me show you the house, and then I'll take you out to the stables." He hesitated. "And then maybe later, or tomorrow…" he trailed off.

"You'd like to start talking strategy," finished Ben. "No problem."

Brian looked relieved, and with it, Ben began to realize just how scared of Nebraska Brian—and probably the rest of the town—really was.

*****

The house wasn't anything special—a small ranch-style, single-story home, probably built in the 1970s. It had two small bedrooms, a living room, and a tiny kitchen. An outhouse had been built out in the back yard.

"How do you keep the lawn from becoming overgrown?" asked Ben.

"We have some push lawnmowers in town, and a couple of guys have taken it upon themselves to be the town's official mowers. We also bring in some of the animals from the farm to eat the grass. Works out well."

"And the woodstove? It looks like it was added recently."

"When we first got here," explained Brian, "we found a few old trucks that weren't affected by the event—you know, pre-computer chip truck."

"Yes, we had one of those, too," said Ben. "I eventually couldn't find any gas for it."

"That happened here, as well, but we got almost three years out of them before they went silent. We brought in everything we could, including woodstoves. All of the garages have been converted to storage areas."

It didn't look to Ben as if the house would need much work. Already, it was more luxurious than the cabin by the lake.

"Let me show you the stables," said Brian.

They left the town by the road they had come in on, but immediately turned right. It was a warm cloudless day, and the mile walk was nothing to them, considering all the traveling they had done.

"You're going to see a lot of horses, Katie," said Brian."

"Can I ride one?" Katie asked.

"Not only can you ride one," answered Brian, "you can have one all your own."

Katie looked up at Ben, as if to confirm what Brian had just said. He nodded his head, resulting in a big smile from his daughter.

Not many weeks earlier, Katie hadn't met another human, other than us. Now, she seemed almost totally at ease around them. She no longer hid behind Lila's legs when we met people. She hadn't yet initiated any conversations, but had no problem replying when spoken to. Another few weeks—or maybe only days—and it would be as if she had always lived around others. This was what Lila had been so anxious to give Katie. Would we still want to leave, come spring?

The stables were spectacular. A few of the townspeople worked there, caring for the horses and cleaning the stalls.

"Some of this farm was already here," said Brian. "We added on to the buildings—luckily we have a few carpenters in town—and can house all of the horses here. All the farms are within a ten-mile radius, so it's not too bad. We split the animals up between them. The horses are here, the smaller animals—like the chickens—are at the second farm. We keep the larger animals like the cattle at the ranch. A few of the town's residents have chosen to live at the stables, the farm, and ranch year-round. They make trips in every few days with the eggs, milk, and meat."

"Sounds like it's a pretty smooth operation," said Lila.

"It works well, and everyone seems happy. As time goes on, I think we miss our old lives less and less. The simplicity of it all is very appealing."

"You don't have to convince us of that," said Ben.

"No, I suppose I don't."

They spent the rest of the day choosing horses and beginning the riding lessons. With the help of the horse experts, Ben picked out a tall chestnut-colored horse. Lila's horse was jet black—Ben was convinced it was because it matched her hair. Katie chose a pinto.

Ben watched Katie closely. At six, would she shy away from the horse, or be anxious to get right into the saddle? She did neither. Instead, she approached the horse slowly, holding out her hand. She touched his nose and started to pet him. She spoke quietly. Ben couldn't hear her words. He looked over at Lila, who was watching Katie just as intently. She looked back at him and smiled. He shook his head in wonder. Instinctively she knew to connect with the animal before attempting to ride it. It was like Katie, he thought, to try to make friends with it. And it was working. The horse nuzzled her, sensing her gentleness.

"What are you going to call him?" asked Ben.

"Oh daddy," scolded Katie. "I just met him. He hasn't told me his name yet."

"Of course," said Ben, stifling a laugh. "What was I thinking?"

Taking a cue from their daughter, Ben and Lila took some time to talk to their mounts as well, letting the horses get used to their scent. Finally, the time came to get into the saddle. Maureen, one of the horse handlers, helped Katie up onto her horse, then instructed Ben and Lila on how to use the stirrups to swing into the saddle. The saddles creaked as they got settled.

"Whoa," said Ben, nervously holding onto the saddle horn. "This horse is taller than I thought." He looked over at Lila. As usual, she didn't seem fazed at all.

Maureen went over the basics of riding and how to control the horse's movements. She then took them for a ride in one of the pastures, first walking, then cantering.

"We'll deal with galloping another time," said Maureen, as they reached the end of their first lesson.

"Thank God it's over," Ben whispered to Lila.

"You didn't like it?" she asked. "I had a great time." She looked over at Katie, who was wearing a big smile. "I think someone else did, too."

"It's not that I didn't like it," said Ben. "I'm just really sore."

"Your butt?"

"More like my, um," he looked at Katie, then leaned closer to Lila, "family jewels. I'm going to be black and blue for a month."

Lila laughed. "You could ride side-saddle."

Ben gave her a dirty look.

Back at the stable, Maureen instructed them on how to take off the saddles and care for the horses. Katie lovingly brushed hers.

"Do you get the feeling that Katie is going to want to spend a lot of time here?" asked Ben.

"She may have found her calling," answered Lila. She then motioned for Ben to come outside. "Do you notice how genuinely happy everyone looks?" she asked when they were away from the others. "It's like they've found a life that they can sink their teeth into. It's peaceful and quiet. After everything that they've been through, they have once again found a home."

"What strikes me," said Ben, "is the difference between this group and all of the people we ran across on our journey south right after the event. People were scared and lost. They missed their old world and didn't know what to make of the new one. These are the survivors, the ones strong enough to make it this far. They either don't miss the old world, or have managed to put it behind them. I guess it makes me feel hopeful that we all have a chance."

They were making their way back to the town a few minutes later when they saw Brian hurrying down the path toward them.

"Uh oh," said Ben. He could tell from Brian's body language that all was not well.

They met up a minute later.

"Something's wrong," said Ben, stating the obvious.

"It is," answered Brian. "We're not going to have as much

time to prepare as I had hoped. An older couple just walked into town from the west. They were grateful to have found us. They've been on the run. Nebraska's out there and coming this way. A large convoy. We're going to have a fight on our hands!

Chapter 14

Lila looked at Ben in alarm. He knew what she was thinking. When it was just the two of them, they could work as a pair. Katie changed everything. He was going to insist that whatever was decided, Lila was going to have to stay with their daughter. He doubted that Lila would put up any objections.

But Lila was ahead of him. "Katie and I will go back into town," she said, anxious for Katie not to overhear too much of the conversation. "We'll take our stuff to our new house and get moved in and try to make it comfortable." She squeezed Ben's hand and went off with Katie and Ralph.

Ben and Brian also walked in the direction of the town.

"How far away are they?" Ben finally asked, when Lila and Katie were out of earshot.

"Three or four days. Maybe more. Big convoy. Twelve or more trucks. Enough for everyone here. There's no doubt where they are headed and what their intentions are."

They both went silent, each chewing on the information. They reached the town and picked up their pace as they headed for Brian's office.

When they arrived, an older man and woman were there, along with two men and a woman Ben hadn't seen before.

"Ben, this is Andrea, Skip, and Steve. They are my unofficial advisors. I run most things by them before presenting ideas to the town."

"Nice to meet you," said Ben, shaking their hands. The men were both in their forties. Skip looked to be a laborer of some kind, big and burly, maybe a carpenter or plumber by trade. Steve had most likely been a corporate drone of some sort in his old life. Although he had a strong upper body now — as did most of the survivors — Ben could tell he hadn't always looked that way. Andrea was younger — around thirty, Ben guessed — and had probably been a graduate student at the time of the event. Not that it did any good to speculate. What people once were was very different from what they had become.

"Welcome to Monett," said Andrea. "Guess you've come at the wrong time."

"Or the right time," said Skip. "Your reputation precedes you."

"Reputations have a way of doing that, I suppose," said Ben with a grimace.

"And this is Dorothy and Tom," said Brian. Ben wondered if there would ever come a time when last names would be used again.

The couple seemed to be in their late-fifties, in good physical shape for their age.

They shook hands and Ben asked, "So you were captives of the Nebraska people?"

EDEN LOST

"We were," answered Tom. "We managed to slip out one night—just a fluke thing, because they usually guarded us well. We were able to disable two of their trucks. They won't go anywhere unless all of the trucks are able to move, so we figured we gained a couple of days from that."

"How many more captives do they have?" asked Brian.

"Ten," said Dorothy. "We were all part of a small settlement. They caught us by surprise. A few people managed to get away, but they got most of us."

"How many people are we going up against?" asked Ben.

"Close to thirty," answered Tom. He must have sensed a confidence coming from some of the group, because he followed it with, "all heavily armed. Thirty may not sound like a major force, but these guys know what they're doing. You have, what, maybe 200 people here?"

"One-sixty-five," replied Brian.

"And a lot of them are children, right? And how many of the adults are fighters—real fighters?"

He was met with silence.

"I'm not trying to be negative, but you've got to understand, these people can take out a town this size in a matter of an hour."

"Anything you can tell us about them?" asked Ben. "Any weaknesses that you observed?"

The couple looked at each other, then shook their heads. "You're not going to like what I'm going to say, but," he hesitated, "you might want to consider not fighting them."

"Are you crazy?" sputtered Skip. "Can you see what we've built here? You want us to give this up? Did they brainwash you?"

117

"No," answered Tom. "I'm only saying that because I've seen what they can do. Even before they captured our group, we were aware of their strength and viciousness. Refusing to go with them isn't an option. If you fight, a lot of people might die, and some of them might be kids caught in the crossfire."

There wasn't much they could say to that.

Tom added, "I don't like their methods, but they might be right about some things. That town they talk about, the one that has electricity, there's something appealing about it. Already most of the folks they took from our settlement want to go there, so they are not really captives anymore."

"So why did you escape?" asked Ben.

"For your sake. We knew this was a pretty big settlement, and we figured you'd elect to fight back. So we thought about it and decided it was more important to warn you to avoid people getting hurt. If you decide to take their offer, Dorothy and I are no worse off than we were before."

Steve offered to take them over to the now-empty guest house and get them situated. Brian thanked them for the information, and they headed out the door with Steve.

"Suggestions?" asked Brian, when they had gone.

"Well, we're certainly not going to give up," said Skip.

"Of course not," said Brian. "So what's the best way to proceed?"

They all looked at Ben. He sighed. Once again he had become the de facto leader.

"Like it or not, they were right about one thing. If they get this far, people could die. So I think the answer is to fight them on our terms. We go after them. Guerrilla warfare. It's always been the most effective form of fighting. We ambush them. We make sure they never make it this far." They talked for another half hour, discussing their options. Finally, Ben said, "We've got a couple of days to plan for it, so I suggest we sleep on it tonight and come back fresh tom..."

Steve had walked in on Ben's last statement. Ben stopped when he saw Steve's face.

"I don't think we have that long," said Steve.

They all stared at him.

"I think we were duped. They just stole a couple of horses and rode out of town."

"Shit!" shouted Brian. "They were gathering information. And I told them exactly how many people we have in town. How could I be so stupid?"

"We all were," said Ben. "We took them at face value. It was naïve on our part. If we'd been in the wilderness, we would have been on alert, but here it's easy to let our guard down."

"So what does it mean?" asked Skip.

"It means they could be on our doorstep tomorrow," said Andrea in disgust. "We should have been suspicious when they showed up on foot. That convoy can't be very far away."

"There is one bit of good news," said Ben. "They made a major mistake." They all looked at him in anticipation.

"They showed their hand. It would have been so easy for Tom and Dorothy to stay here and work to sabotage us from the inside. Or, if nothing else, stay a while longer until they knew our plans, then take off. By leaving now, they've tipped us off to the fact that Nebraska is a lot closer than they indicated."

"So what do we do?" asked Steve.

"We do what Ben suggested," said Brian. "We don't let them penetrate the town. We attack them before they get here. Steve, go to the tower and tell whoever is up there to keep an eye out for any movement. We don't know where they are, but we have to assume they are close by."

"How many people do we have who can fight?" asked Ben.

"About twenty people live out on the farms. When we subtract them, the kids, and the adults who have to care for the kids, that leaves eighty or so."

"We'll have to leave a force here, just in case, and maybe send a few out to reinforce the farms—again, just in case," said Ben.

"That gives us about fifty," said Skip. "That should be enough to take out thirty of them."

"If there are really only thirty," observed Andrea.

"I don't think they were lying about that," said Ben. "If anything, they might have exaggerated the number to get us to consider surrendering. I saw a convoy. Granted, it was smaller, but they had two to a truck. Assuming the same here, plus a few extra to guard prisoners, I'd say thirty would be the max."

"Andrea," ordered Brian. "You need to go ring the bell."

"On my way," she said, and was out the door.

Brian turned to Ben. "We have an emergency bell. When it rings, people come running. We should have everyone outside this building in ten minutes."

Brian overestimated the time. The space in front of the town office was packed in less than five. Someone had alerted Lila, and she was right in front with Katie and Ralph. Ben called her over to the side and quickly filled her in.

"I want to be a part of it," she said quietly so Katie couldn't hear, "but obviously I need to stay here with Katie."

"You do. But you can probably help organize the town, just in case they make it past us."

Ben moved over to Brian.

"Lila's going to stay here, but as you know, she is battle-trained. So anything she can do, she will."

"Actually, I'm going to put her in charge. There won't be any objections. Everybody knows her experience. They will appreciate having her here to lead."

Brian called the meeting to order and proceeded to divvy up the responsibilities. Those heading out to the farms for added protection left as soon as their names were called. He introduced Lila to the group—many of whom hadn't yet met her—and explained that she was going to help get the town fortified.

"As for the rest of us, those who don't have your horses here need to get over to the stable and saddle up."

Ben froze. He had only had one lesson. Brian caught the movement. "Don't worry," he whispered. "We won't be doing any galloping. You might learn more about your horse today than you would in a dozen lessons."

He addressed the crowd again. "Grab your weapons and plenty of ammunition. We may be busy."

"What's the plan?" someone yelled from the crowd.

"We don't have a plan yet, but we will. We'll figure it out on the fly. We meet back here in an hour, mounted and ready to go."

Ben walked with his family to the house to retrieve his rifle and crossbow.

"I won't say it" said Lila.

"I won't either. We've been through a lot of battles. We know how to take care of ourselves. We'll come through this just like we always have."

They hugged and shared a long, passionate kiss.

"Come back safe," said Lila.

"Thought you weren't going to say it," said Ben with a grin.

"Couldn't help myself."

"Take care of our girl," said Ben, lifting Katie and giving her a big kiss.

"Be careful, daddy."

"I will, honey," answered Ben, amazed once again at her ability to perceive what was going on.

He made his way back to the meeting place, the familiar feel of the rifle and crossbow slung over his back. He arrived at about the same time as most of the others. He looked around at the townspeople.

I saw determination in those faces. Such a far cry from most of the people we ran across seven years earlier. These were people who had fought their way through some of the worst a person could experience. And they had made it when so many others had given up and lost hope. Even if they hadn't had to fire their weapon at another human being, even if they hadn't had to take another life, it didn't matter. They were fighting for the life they had carved out for themselves. It was beyond courage. They were willing to fight for their right to live, and there was no one else I would want next to me in battle.

As a group, they walked the mile to the stables. Ben was nervous—not about the battle to come, but about the prospect of riding the horse. He was already so sore it was uncomfortable to walk. What if he couldn't control the horse?

"Seriously," said Brian, reading his thoughts. "You'll be fine. You'll remember more from that lesson than you think."

"Do I have some sort of billboard on my head flashing my thoughts?" asked Ben. "Lila does that to me all the time. I think I've got to be careful what I think."

Brian laughed, then quickly turned serious. "Any predictions?"

"It all depends on how close they are and how much time we have to prepare." He looked around. "These people are willing. But are they skilled enough to go up against something like this? I guess we'll find out."

One of the stable hands brought out Ben's horse and helped him saddle it.

Here we go, thought Ben, as he pulled himself up into the saddle. The horse was steady, as if it recognized a neophyte in the saddle.

"Let's get to it," shouted Brian, and they all started off.

Ben counted. Forty-one men and fourteen women, all looking somber. There were no cowboys in this lot. A job needed to be done. No one was happy about it, but they were all ready to do what they had to.

He just had to keep thoughts of General Custer and the Little Big Horn out of his head.

Chapter 15

They turned left when they exited the town. It brought them through the remains of what used to be Monett, Missouri, now overgrown. Very few intact buildings remained. Those the fire hadn't destroyed, the earthquake had finished. There were deep fissures in the concrete—in some places no concrete at all—but Brian led them through. Ben could see a well-worn path.

"Guess you've been out here a lot," he said. He was riding in the front of the group next to Brian, very self-conscious of what the others might be thinking about his riding. It occurred to him that he hadn't felt that self-conscious since before the event. After all I've been through, I'm worried about how I look? he thought to himself. After having that thought, he no longer cared, and could focus on the task at hand.

"Can't tell you how many times we've been this way scouting over the years."

"How did you know to turn left and go through the town, rather than right and past the farm? Are you sure they'll come this way?"

"Positive. We have to assume they are coming from the northwest. Because of the terrain and the new canyons, it would take them five times as long to go around the other way. No, this is the most advantageous route for them. So my question for you is, when's the best time to confront them?"

"Preferably never. Usually night is a good time, but I have a feeling we're going to meet up with them before then. Also, with twelve trucks, they might even make camp like the old settlers and put their trucks in a circle, giving them a tremendous amount of protection."

"But if we meet them while they're still traveling, they can plow through us. They might have some sort of protection covering the windshields."

"Then we go for the tires," said Ben, with a germ of an idea. He fleshed it out as he talked. "They have to go single-file. There are some wide open areas, but we have to figure that for the most part, they'll be in a line. Ideally, we get them if they reach a ravine they have to put their bridge across. When the first truck is halfway over, we go for the tires and get the truck stuck on the bridge. If we can get close enough, we try to destroy the bridge. If we catch up to them when they're not going over a ravine, we go with the same plan and get the tires. Without their trucks, they are more vulnerable than we are."

They rode in silence for another hour, each lost in his thoughts, but constantly on the lookout for a sign of Nebraska. They had been following a fairly intact piece of road, but were now off it, going through farm country.

"I know why Tom and Dorothy left when they did," Ben said suddenly. It was the answer to a question that had been nagging at him for a few miles.

"Those assholes," muttered Brian, more angry at himself for not seeing through the couple's charade.

"They were scouting the easiest path into the town," said Ben. "Nebraska needed someone to scout the way, and by sending in Tom and Dorothy, they accomplished that—as well as finding out how strong we were."

"Why didn't they just try to take us by surprise?" asked Brian. "Why warn us like that?"

"Hey Brian," one of the group called out. "Does it look to you that there are some tire tracks here?"

Ben stopped his horse. "Oh, shit!" he exclaimed. "This is why! I can't believe how stupid I've been. They warned us so we would come out in search of them. They knew it wouldn't do any good for us to make a stand in the town. We wouldn't stand a chance. They knew we'd form a posse and try to head them off. They tricked us. They've split us up. We made it easier for them. We probably passed right by them. They're on their way to the town right now!"

Brian turned his horse around and quickly passed the information on to the others. There was a lot of swearing. They reversed direction as one—reminiscent of a flock of birds—and started galloping back toward the town. Ben was about to get a crash course on hard riding.

I was self-sufficient. I could handle myself in many different situations. But I never wanted to be a leader, and this proved to me that I wasn't. While my idea of guerrilla warfare was sound, I realized that I didn't have the make-up of a leader. Granted, we didn't have a lot of time, but I should have taken more time to explore the possibilities. If I'd really thought about it, I might have put two and two together and realized that this was their plan all along. But I didn't, and now some people might die. Brian was happy I had shown up, knowing he could look to me for advice. I couldn't have given him any worse advice.

This time Ben was at the rear of the pack. His lack of riding skills was hampering his progress. The group had left him far behind. Even Brian, who had been so supportive, had more important things to think about now. Ben cursed himself for being so inept on his horse, wishing he had had more time to practice. Lila and Katie were in danger and he couldn't do anything about it. The only saving grace was that he believed Nebraska wanted people alive to bring back. There was no reason to kill, unless they encountered resistance. Of course, if anyone was going to resist, it would be Lila. She had vowed never to be imprisoned again—and that would be the last thing she would want for Katie.

His horse was in a trot. He tried to remember how to make it go faster. Suddenly, on its own, it picked up speed. Maybe it just wanted to keep up with the other horses. It broke into a gallop and Ben hung on for dear life. He remembered hearing a story of some actor who had fallen off his horse and was paralyzed for the rest of his life. He thought he remembered hearing that the guy played Superman in an old movie. How ironic. Nevertheless, it was that thought, combined with the urgency of getting back to his family, that kept Ben on his horse. He was sure it wasn't pretty, but he didn't care about that now.

His horse was big and strong, and in a few minutes had caught up with some of the slower riders. He shot past them, much to their amazement. The horse only slowed down a fraction when it reached the rest of the group.

When they got within a couple of miles of the town, they all slowed down to a trot, suddenly realizing that they had no idea what they would do when they arrived.

Ben found himself next to Brian again.

"Suggestions?" asked Brian.

"From me? Haven't I screwed things up enough?"

"No one blames you," said Brian. "We all had a hand in the decision. It was the smart thing to do, considering the circumstances. We just didn't realize they were so close."

"Well, I still think we need to go for the tires first," said Ben, feeling marginally better. "It will slow them down enough so we can start picking them off. It just depends how close to the town they made it."

The horses in front of them slowed to a stop.

"Brian, look," said Skip.

Coming from the direction of the town was a large column of thick black smoke.

Chapter 16

(Lila)

Everything had happened so quickly. One minute Lila and Katie were setting up their new house, and the next minute they were saying goodbye to Ben. Very few instructions were given, other than that Lila was supposed to help prepare the town in case of attack. She guessed that this honor was bestowed upon her by virtue of her experience in battle. Did violence just follow them wherever they went? Monett had been a happy little community for a few years. Enter Ben and Lila and suddenly they were at war. She remembered her grandfather once telling her about a comic-strip character years before who always had a black rain cloud over his head. It had stayed with her because she thought it was a funny image. She understood it now. She and Ben together were that character.

Well, like it or not, she was here, and people were counting on her. She looked around. The rest of the town was still gathered in front of the town office. All eyes were on her. She suddenly realized that while her experience had something to do with the respect she was being shown, more of it had to do with her appearance. With the black patch and the small, but memorable scar, she looked like Lila, Queen of the Pirates.

"What do you suggest?" asked Sharon. "I don't think most of us have ever experienced anything quite like this. Frankly," she lowered her voice for the children's sake, "we're pretty scared."

Lila looked around. Mostly women and children. Some men remained, but they tended to be the older ones.

"I don't think we have a lot to worry about," she said in a voice all could hear. "I seriously doubt they would make it this far. But we should be prepared for that off-chance. I think we should have as few people as possible here in the town. I think the kids should be moved out of town. They should be taken to the stable to get their horses, then they should go to one of the farms further out. Chances are these people don't know anything about those farms. Parents should accompany the kids, and the only people left here should be those without kids. How many is that?"

Hands went up. Lila counted fifteen. "Okay, that's the force to guard the town."

"Is that going to be enough?" someone asked.

"It should be, if we do it right."

From the back of the group came a woman's voice. "Who put you in charge?"

Sharon turned in disgust to the woman. It was obvious to Lila that this was not the woman's first altercation with the group.

"Shut up, Elizabeth," said Sharon. "We don't need this right now."

"All I'm saying is that this Lila person is new to the town. Why should we listen to her?"

Before Sharon could answer, Lila spoke up.

"You're right. There's no reason for me to be in charge. I don't even want the job. So why don't you take over. It's your show now."

She had used that technique a couple of times in high school when dealing with big-mouthed know-it-alls. It was usually enough to shut them up. Once again, it worked.

"I wasn't saying I wanted to be in charge," said Elizabeth. "I was just questioning why we should be listening to her, that's all." Her voice had lost its punch.

"Because we want to," said Walt. He looked at her. "Have you ever been in a battle for your life?" She shook her head. "Well, this girl has … numerous times." He motioned to Lila, now that Elizabeth had been put in her place. "Please continue."

"I think everyone with kids should leave now. Don't stop to get anything, or just grab something from your house only if it's really essential. Get to the horses and go to one of the outlying farms. Sharon, could you take care of Katie?"

The thought of being separated from her daughter killed her, but she knew she had to keep her safe.

"I'd be happy to."

Katie grabbed one of Lila's legs. "No, mommy, I'm not going. I want to be with you."

"It would be safer, sweetie."

"No! We're a team," she said, echoing something both Ben and Lila had said to her many times in the past. "I have to stay with you."

Katie had brought up a good point. We had always done things as a family—as a team. Was it right to change that now? Would she really be any safer with that group than she would be with me? And what about me? Could I keep my attention on the task at hand worrying about Katie? What if she fell off her horse? After all, she was still new at riding. What if ... what if anything. She wanted to be in the center of the action. In that way she took after both of us. No, I had to keep her with me. I thought Ben would agree. Anyway, I doubted we'd even see the Nebraska group.

"Katie's right, Sharon. I think it's best if she stays with me. She'll be okay."

Sharon understood and began ushering the kids toward the town entrance. She stopped and turned to Lila.

"Good luck."

"Good luck to you too. I know the kids are in good hands."

Sharon came back and gave Lila a hug. She tapped the gun at her side. "We may not look like much, and maybe we don't have much battle experience, but just let them try to mess with us. You don't threaten a bunch of momma bears and their cubs." She gave a smile and turned away.

You've got that right, thought Lila.

Including Katie, there were eighteen of them. Six women, eleven older men, and one child against a force of thirty or more fighting men.

I'd seen better odds.

One minute there was the noise and confusion of the parents leaving with their children, and the next, complete silence.

"I'm open to suggestions," said Lila, breaking the silence. "Any of you guys serve in the military?"

Seven of them raised their hands.

"Any with combat experience?"

They all shook their head.

"I served in Vietnam," said a man of about seventy, "but I was stationed at a base and didn't see any action."

"I never saw combat," said Walt, "but if you don't mind, I have a suggestion."

"Please," she waved him on.

"Seems to me that if they happen to show up and no one is here to greet them, it'll leave 'em at a loss."

"Are you saying we should leave?" asked one of the other men.

"No. Just give the appearance of it. We pick some houses along the street. We become snipers. They come in all cocky and ready to take over, only to find no one to here take over. If we have to fight, we have the advantage from the houses. I suggest two to a house—the first houses as they enter the town, four on one side, five on the other. If we're lucky, we can take them without firing a shot. And if we do have to fight, we've got 'em in a crossfire." He looked at Lila. "That work for you?"

"Works for me. I suggest we go gather all the fire power we have and meet back here in a few minutes." She motioned for Walt to stay behind.

"Thank you for the suggestion," she said, when the others had left. "I feel a little awkward. All of a sudden everyone was looking to me. Elizabeth was a loud-mouth, but she was right. Who put me in charge? And why? I only know a few people here."

"Don't kid yourself," said Walt. "When a teenage girl carves out the legend that you did, people take note. And you're not a teenager anymore, so you probably have a certain added wisdom that you didn't have before to go along with your courage, experience, and abilities. Someone like you only comes along in folklore, so when presented with the real thing, people will listen."

He thought for a minute, then continued. "Don't ever doubt your leadership abilities. Those of us who are left in this world may be the strong ones, but it doesn't mean we don't still look for inspiration. We need the stories, and the legends, and the folklore to keep us going, to show us that we're going in the right direction. You've got the humility that marks a good leader, but don't be afraid to bark out an order from time to time. Believe it or not, they want that. Sometimes they crave it." Lightening up, he looked down at Katie and said, "And I can already tell you take after your mother. You listen to her and you'll be a leader too."

There was a part of me that didn't want Katie to be a leader, but then I realized that Walt was right. People wanted leaders. Katie already had the instincts and the courage. In a few years—much earlier than it was for me—she would command respect just by her very presence.

They parted to go to their respective houses to pick up their weapons. Lila loaded her rifle and put a box of shells in a backpack. She put a couple of extra magazines for her pistol in her jacket pocket.

"Mommy," Katie came into the room lugging her crossbow. "Should I bring my crossbow?"

"No, honey. I think you can leave that here. I'm very proud of your shooting, but we won't need that today. It's going to be very important that you stay out of sight of the windows when we guard the other house. Do you understand?"

"Okay." She looked crestfallen.

Lila gave her a hug. "The reason is, we need your crossbow for hunting. You're the best hunter we have. As soon as all this is over, you and daddy can go and hunt us some meals."

That perked Katie up, so they finished filling Lila's backpack and made their way back to the town office. The others were already there.

"We were just talking," said Walt. "How would you feel if the sixteen of us take the first four houses on each side, and you and Katie take the fifth house on your preferred side of the street. You being probably the best shot here can be our ace in the hole. You can pick them off one by one if they make it past us."

It wasn't much of a plan, but Lila knew the reasons behind it. They wanted Katie as far from the action as possible. Truth was, Lila probably was the best shot there, and putting her the furthest distance away made sense.

The house she took was fifth in line on the left-hand side of the road for anyone entering the town. Lila didn't know who it belonged to, but they had done a nice job of decorating it. It was a house with children, as one of the bedrooms was filled with toys. Lila liked the house because it jutted out slightly, giving her a clear view of the whole street.

With Katie playing with some of the toys at her feet, Lila sat in a chair by the window waiting for something that would probably never come.

That theory was shattered an hour later when they heard the rumbling of trucks.

"Shit," said Lila under her breath. "Okay, Katie, I need you and Ralph to go into the room with the toys. Even if you hear my rifle, don't come out, okay?"

Katie got up and gave her a big hug. "Okay, mommy. Be careful."

"I will, sweetie. Don't worry."

"I'm not. Come on, Ralph."

When they had gone in and closed the door, Lila took out her ammo and set it down on the floor below the window. Her rifle was a Bushmaster that carried a clip of four bullets. She had a pile of extra magazines filled with bullets and ready to go, in case she had to do a lot of shooting.

Lila wondered what had happened to Ben and the posse, and how they could have missed them. It was a moot point. It was now their responsibility.

The trucks began to enter the town. The first vehicle was a Jeep with two occupants. It took five minutes for the slow-moving trucks to come through the gate, the lead vehicle stopping in front of the fourth house in line. They turned off their engines and the street went quiet. Dorothy and Tom had exaggerated. It wasn't twelve, it was only eight: the Jeep, some kind of armored vehicle, the tanker truck with the bridge strapped to the top, four large canvas-topped trucks, and another Jeep bringing up the rear. The Jeeps each had a large machine gun in the back with someone manning it. Surprisingly, the armored vehicle didn't have any noticeable weapons, but it did have portholes in the side, probably for the men inside to shoot out of.

Seeing nobody around, the first Jeep started to honk its horn. The two men in the front seat stood up to have a better look around. One of them was Tom.

"What'd you do, scare them away?" asked the driver. "You were supposed to get them to surrender when we showed up, not run away."

"They're just hiding," said Tom. "They put too much work into this town to run. They're around here somewhere." He raised his hand and suddenly the street was full of men. Lila did a quick count and came up with twenty-two. Add whoever was in the armored vehicle and the number was probably closer to twenty-five. He called out. "Hey everybody! Look, I warned you. You are over-matched. You don't want any of your kids hurt. Don't make a fight of it. You won't win."

Lila knew now that a fight was exactly what they were going to get. She went over to the room Katie was in.

"Katie. Change of plans. I need you to go into the bathroom and get in the tub." Lila had noticed the bathroom had an old-fashioned clawfoot iron tub. "Lie down inside it with Ralph."

Katie quickly obeyed and Lila dragged out a mattress from

the kids' room and laid it over the top of the tub. The iron would hold off any bullets coming directly in, and she hoped the mattress would protect her against ricochets. She was now seriously regretting not sending Katie away.

"What was I thinking?" she mumbled as she got back to the window.

The men started to move up the street.

"Okay, Walt," she said to herself. "It's now or never."

Almost as if he heard her, a shot sounded, followed by a second. A moment later, a cacophony of gunshots filled the air. A few of the men in the street fell to the ground. Others dropped down to fire, or ran to one of the trucks for protection. The initial volley hadn't taken as many of them out as she would have hoped—maybe four or five. She knew from experience that shooting in the heat of battle didn't tend to yield very accurate results. She held off firing until she had a clear shot.

The shooting died out momentarily. Tom took that opportunity to call out. "Cease fire! Stop your shooting!" Everyone on both sides held off, waiting to hear what he would say.

"Listen a minute. Yeah, you got a few of us, but you won't now. We're all pretty well hidden. So this can go on for a long time. And we have another convoy right behind us with double the men."

That's a lie, thought Lila.

"Believe it or not, we're doing this for your own good. Our city has power. It has all the conveniences you once had. And it's growing. You can all live comfortable lives again."

"We're comfortable here," said Walt. "And you come in

here with armored trucks, machine guns, and heavily armed men, and you expect us to believe you?"

"That's just to protect ourselves."

"Yeah, right. We don't want you here, so go away."

Tom's voice took on a different tone.

"Then here's some added incentive for you to give up. We have ten hostages. We'll start killing them one at a time until you call it quits."

"Why should we care?" called out Walt.

"Because you're civilized. You don't want innocent people to die. There's no way you can win this."

"Aren't you defeating the purpose of gathering people by killing some?"

"Sometimes sacrifices have to be made."

At that moment, Dorothy climbed out the back of the second canvas-covered truck with a woman as a shield. The hostage was young—a teenager—and Dorothy had a gun to the girl's head.

"You have thirty seconds to lay down your weapons, or that girl dies," Tom commanded.

Chapter 17

"Can you really live with that on your conscience?" said Tom.

Lila noticed that even though Tom was doing all the talking, he wasn't in charge. The other one in the Jeep—the driver—was quietly calling the shots from the background. He was the one she had to take out. With him gone, the rest would have to make decisions for themselves, and she didn't think that would happen. In this case though, she would have to take out both the leader and Tom, who was the obvious second-in-command.

"Twenty seconds."

It was up to her. She knew the others would follow her lead.

"Fifteen seconds."

She couldn't let the girl die.

She laid her rifle on the sill of the open window. She had yet to shoot, so they wouldn't be expecting it from that house.

"Ten seconds. C'mon people."

She lined up Dorothy in her sights, using her good left eye.

The moment of truth, she thought.

"Five seconds."

She fired. The teenager screamed and dropped from a stunned Dorothy's arms.

"Shit, shit, shit," cried Lila. She had hit the hostage. She quickly took aim again and fired. This time the bullet caught Dorothy, who no longer had her human shield, in the center of her chest. She fell to the ground, a puddle of blood quickly forming around her.

"No!" yelled Tom, who stood up from behind the Jeep.

Lila redirected her rifle and hit Tom in the upper chest. The leader of the group, not expecting fire from Lila's building, had left himself somewhat exposed from Lila's direction. He turned to jump behind the Jeep. She fired and caught him in the butt. He jumped in pain as she quickly changed magazines. She put two more bullets into him before he could scramble over the side of the Jeep, and he went down.

Meanwhile, the battle in the street had started up again. A couple more men fell, but the others were fairly well hidden. The machine guns were silent. The two men manning the large guns were the first to fall in the initial shooting and no one had taken their places.

Suddenly, a bright light almost blinded Lila, and she went momentarily deaf, before hearing the "whump" of something blowing up. The blast blew her from her spot in the window. She fell to the floor, dazed. Slowly, she came to her senses and shakily got to her feet. The ringing in her ears was intense and a black smoke filled the air. She made her way to the bathroom to check on Katie. She and Ralph were fine.

"Stay in here."

"What was that, mommy?" asked Katie, but Lila didn't hear her and went back to the window.

Through the smoke she could see the tanker truck—or what was left of it—smoldering in the center of the street. The remaining Nebraska crew were wandering around, holding their ears, no longer carrying their weapons. The armored truck directly in front, and the canvas-covered truck directly behind the tanker were also destroyed. She could see hostages falling out the back of the second canvas-covered truck. But everything seemed in slow-motion.

Finally, she had enough of her senses to venture outside. Others from her group were doing the same. One by one, the stragglers from the convoy were rounded up and told to lie on the ground. They gave no fight. They had no fight left in them.

Lila figured that some bullets must have punctured the tanker, spilling the fuel. Some ricochets probably sparked a fire, leading to the explosion. But it was only speculation.

Other than the ringing, Lila was almost back to normal. She ran over to the hostage truck to check on the girl she hit with the bullet.

"Oh God, please let her be okay," cried Lila as she ran.

The girl was hurt, but was far from dead. Lila's bullet had caught her in the left bicep. She was bleeding profusely, but Lila knew she would live. The explosion had done almost as much damage to her, as she was bleeding from lacerations to her head. Walt had also made her his first destination. He took off his shirt and made a makeshift bandage out of it for her arm. The head wounds were superficial.

"Always looks worse than it is," he said to Lila. "That was really good shooting."

"What do you mean? I hit the hostage."

"Of course you did. It was going to take a pretty miraculous shot from that distance not to. But you didn't kill her. I'm talking about your next shots: Dorothy, Tom, and then the leader. Precision shots. And I heard that you had to relearn how to shoot after you lost your right eye. That couldn't have been easy."

There was nothing Lila could say to that, so she touched Walt in thanks, then went to survey the rest of the scene.

Other than a couple of minor wounds, the Monett residents fared well. All of the hostages, ten in all including the girl Lila shot—at least Tom and Dorothy weren't lying about that— were okay. Someone was giving them water.

She counted seventeen dead Nebraskans. Four more had serious wounds, leaving only six unhurt. One of the Monett residents tied their hands and legs, and sat them at the edge of the street.

Lila went to get Katie. She had been in the bathtub long enough. When Lila pulled the mattress off the top, she found a hot, sweaty child, and an equally warm dog. She led them out to the not-so-fresh air on the street.

"Try not to look at the dead people, Katie."

"Okay," replied Katie. But Lila knew she couldn't stop her. She knew nothing could stop a child's curiosity. As sick as it was, seeing the bodies was probably a good experience in this new world.

Walt called out to one of the women. "Can you head over to the stables and have them send someone out to the other farms with the news that they can come back? And could you have them get Doc back here as soon as possible? He needs to look at this girl."

It was over. Their motley crew of seventeen had won the fight with more than two dozen heavily armed men. As the realization began to set in, the townspeople started to congratulate each other.

As well they should, thought Lila.

They each commended Lila on her shooting and her leadership. Walt's words before the battle ran through her head. She vowed never again to entertain any doubts about her decision-making and leadership abilities.

A little while later, the posse rode in. She could tell from the worn-out horses that they had been riding hard.

Ben trotted up to her and painfully slid off his horse, obviously relieved to be on solid ground again.

"I can't leave you for a minute without you getting in trouble," he said with a deadpan face. "I can't wait to hear this story!"

"The question is," replied Lila. "How did these guys get past you?"

Ben frowned. "My fault. I was too cocky. I didn't think things through. My mistake almost cost a lot of lives."

"No," said Lila. "It just happened. Don't blame yourself." She repeated what Walt had said to her, and added, "Ben, you're going to make mistakes from time to time, but unlike some, you'll own up to them. We're both going to make mistakes, so we need to get used to it. So they outsmarted you—not just you, though, all of you—it happens." Lila had the beginnings of a smile. "But, as usual, you had me to bail you out."

Ben gave her a hug. "I did, didn't I?"

The cleanup took hours. The prisoners were escorted to a large shed for safekeeping. The church was converted into a make-shift hospital and the wounded were made comfortable while they waited for the doctor. The dead Nebraskans were carried out of the town and temporarily put into an abandoned shell of a building in the old section of the original town. The members of the posse took on new roles without any urging. Half of them immediately started to repair the heavily damaged houses, while the other half worked on the disposal of the three destroyed vehicles. As they worked, the townspeople began to filter in, staring almost as one at the battle remains. The working vehicles were parked outside the entrance to the town.

"What do you suggest we do with the prisoners?" Brian asked Ben.

"We can try to get information from them, but we have no idea if they will even tell the truth, so that will most likely be a wasted exercise."

"Do we let them go?" Brian seemed uncomfortable. Ben knew that Brian thought Ben was going to suggest killing them. Again the reputation.

"We kinda have to." Relief formed on Brian's face. Ben continued, "We don't want to have to guard them indefinitely, so I say we let them go—without weapons, of course. We warn them what will happen if they return."

"Yeah," said Brian, with a slight smirk. "We'll sic Lila on them."

Ben smiled. "A fate worse than death." He turned serious. "What are you going to do with the remaining trucks? I suggest we keep them and use them as work vehicles."

"I don't think the townspeople will agree to that."

"Why not?" Ben was mystified.

"Hard to explain. We've carved out a life here without our former conveniences. When gas became scarce and we gave up our trucks, nobody seemed to mind. I think they were ready to say goodbye to the old world. Besides, the gas problem hasn't improved any."

"One of the trucks has a good number of full gas cans— probably insurance in case something happened to the tanker. So we could get a lot of use out of them until the gas ran out."

Brian was shaking his head. "Nope. I'll bring it up to the townspeople for a vote, but I can guarantee it'll get voted down. The fact is, we like our life here."

"I don't understand it."

"You lived for six years in the forest. I would think you, of all people, would understand."

"We didn't have a choice, and we lived alone. Your situation is different. You're trying to rebuild a civilization. How do you expect to do that without power?"

"We're not trying to rebuild a whole civilization. We're trying to make a life for ourselves, and we like our life here." He could tell Ben wasn't convinced. "Our life is simple. It's like ..." he was searching for the words. "It's like trying to merge two completely different cultures into one. It can't be done. At least, it can't be done so everyone is satisfied. We've figured out how to do everything the simplest way, and we've all embraced it. Those who couldn't embrace it chose to leave a long time ago. Yes, we could spend our time pursuing ways to bring back our old existence, but to what end? Where would it stop? Our world was so technologically advanced, we'd never be able to catch up to what we once had, so we'd always be wanting more. This way, we don't crave more because we don't need it. We have everything necessary right here. What was your impression of Monett when you first arrived?"

Ben didn't have to think. He knew what the answer was. "How happy everyone seemed."

"Exactly. And it's not a false happiness—like they are trying to make the best of it—but a true contentment, Ben. We've moved on from the old world. You have as well. You couldn't have lived so long in the forest without reaching that same conclusion."

Brian finished, "You could look at it as just using the trucks to make life a little easier. No big deal, right? We look at it as an intrusion. Simple as that."

*****

As expected, the prisoners weren't talking, and true to his word, Brian informed them that they would be let go. Also as expected, they complained about being freed with no weapons or mode of transportation. It was decided that the four injured Nebraskans—none of whom had suffered life-threatening wounds—would be let go when they were all ready to travel, separately from the first group.

Ben suggested a final use for the trucks that Brian approved: The first group of prisoners would be taken as far as the trucks could go—until they ran across a wide ravine a few miles away that Brian knew of—and let go. The trucks, in turn, would be pushed into the ravine—as Ben had done with the other group they encountered. Nobody in town wanted a reminder of the Nebraskans' presence, so it was decided that the dead would also travel in the trucks, and the bodies would be thrown into the ravine.

"Here's the thing," Brian said to the prisoners after they were loaded into the truck. "If you ever make it back to your town, let whoever is in charge know that we just want to live in peace. I don't know what your plan is. Maybe it's as simple as wanting to conquer as much territory as possible, which is stupid. But maybe it's something else altogether. Regardless, we will fight. Who knows, maybe you can get the best of us, but it would take an awful lot of you to do it, and your casualties would be excessive. It's just not worth it, no matter what your plan. So take that back with you. We'll always be ready."

Ben drove one of the trucks, and others followed the trucks on horseback, trailing along horses for the men driving the trucks. The prisoners were released, and the dead and the trucks sent to the depths of the ravine. Their task finished, they headed back toward Monett.

I turned in the saddle and watched the sorry procession of Nebraskans walk along the edge of the ravine in their quest to find a way across and head back toward their home. I was sure we'd never have any problems with them again, but I couldn't help thinking that somewhere down the line, we weren't finished with the Nebraska crowd.

Chapter 18

Life settled down for Ben and Lila. They busied themselves getting their house in order and integrating into town life. But deep down they both knew that it wasn't for them. They participated in town activities, both business and social, attended church on Sunday, and enrolled Katie in school. They gave socialization their best shot, but while they appreciated having the opportunity to be around others, it was more interaction than they wanted. They had just spent too much time alone. Over the next few months they had many conversations that all ended the same way—come spring, they would leave.

Even Katie seemed antsy. She got along with the other children and enjoyed school, but the minute school ended for the day, she was back at the stable. When she wasn't riding her horse, she was brushing him, feeding him, and just loving him. A bond formed between them in no time, which came as no surprise to Ben and Lila.

Almost two weeks after the attack, the three of them

decided to go for a family ride to explore the area. Katie had already become comfortable on her horse, and some of the stable hands predicted that she would be an accomplished rider in no time. Although not as comfortable as Katie, Lila was also getting used to riding.

Ben hadn't sat on his horse since the attack, using the excuse that he was still sore "down there."

"Funny," Lila said, "that it hasn't stopped you from 'other' activities."

It was a bright sunny day, warm for mid-autumn. They had endured two days of violent downpours earlier in the week and needed to get out of the house and go somewhere. The ground had dried and Lila convinced Ben that it would be a perfect day to get away for a while.

They reached the stable and sought out their horses.

"C'mon Scooby," said Katie, leading her horse over to the saddles.

Ben and Lila looked at each other.

"Scooby?" Lila asked Katie.

"That's his name." answered Katie matter-of-factly.

"How did you pick that name?" asked Ben.

"I think he looks like Scooby-Doo."

Katie's two favorite shirts were the Scooby-Doo and SpongeBob shirts they had picked out for her.

"I suppose it makes sense that she would name him that," said Lila.

"Better than SpongeBob, anyway," answered Ben. "I suppose we should name our horses."

"I've already thought of that," said Lila. "I've had a name going through my head for a couple of days." She led her horse out of the stable. He had an unruly black mane that gave him a wild look.

"I'm going to call him Captain Jack."

Ben raised an eyebrow.

"He looks a little like Captain Jack Sparrow, and since people seem to think I look like a pirate with my patch, it seems appropriate. Also," she said in a conspiratorial tone, "not to get you jealous, but I always had a thing for Johnny Depp."

"No problem. The list of actresses I had a crush on was pretty long. But in the end, it's you and me."

"So what are you naming yours?"

"Well, he's big and powerful, so I think I'll name him Moose."

"Moose?"

"First-baseman for the Red Sox. Hit forty home runs his rookie year and was on a pace to hit fifty his second year when the season got cut short."

"Why did it get cut short?"

"Um ... the world ended?"

"Oh, that. But Moose?"

"Moose Monaghan. Big guy with bright red hair. Built like a truck."

"And his name was Moose?"

"I'm sure it wasn't his real name. Probably a nickname."

"I would hope."

They got their horses saddled and took off down the road in the direction of the two farms, Ralph following behind. It was a country road that had once been asphalt, and under the many layers of dirt the asphalt was probably still intact, but now it had become a pretty dirt lane. There were cracks in the earth, but for the most part, the earthquake had spared it, and it was a fairly straight run to the farms. Before reaching the first farm, though, Lila spied a small animal trail leading off into the woods a few hundred yards off to their left.

"Want to try it?" she asked.

Ben was feeling more comfortable and agreed. Frankly, he felt he needed it. He needed a reminder of their journey together, so much of which was spent traveling through woods.

It turned out that they hadn't picked an animal trail. Once in the woods, they saw signs for trails.

"This was a park, or a nature preserve at one time," said Lila. "We might get lucky with the trails."

And they did. The trail led to a pristine stream that emerged from a large rock formation. The peace and quiet served its purpose for Ben. They got down off their horses and sat by the water.

"Bring back memories?" he asked Lila.

"Doesn't it seem like so long ago?" she answered. "It was an exciting, but scary time."

Katie had heard watered down versions of some of their adventures south after the event, so she quietly listened, leaning up against Ralph.

"Of all the people we met, who do you miss the most?" asked Ben.

"I really liked Nick and Jason, but I'm pretty sure we'll see them again, so they don't count for me. I'd have to say Phil."

Phil was a young Catholic priest they met early in their journey, when they were still terrified of the new world around them. Phil had created a safe haven for survivors, but one that saw little use. There were so few survivors—especially in the mountains of Western Massachusetts—that there was little need for his services. But Phil was ever the optimist, having spent years helping the poor in third-world countries. They tried to convince him to accompany them, but he chose to stay with his converted church. But when the church burned to the ground during a lightning storm, it proved to be too much for him. Seeing his usefulness fall away, his faith quickly followed, and he committed suicide.

"Phil was one of the truly good people in this world," Lila continued. "He had an outlook on life that was sorely needed in those years after the event—still needed, for that matter. I think he would have been a great friend to us and an important voice in this new society."

"I agree with you," said Ben. "We met some people we liked, but Phil had the greatest heart of all."

Suddenly the mood had become somber. They were ready to leave. They climbed back onto their horses and found the trail back out of the woods. As they were trotting along the road, Ben said, "You know, when I'm not trying to hang on for dear life, I really like horseback riding."

The first farm they came to was a real working farm. Scaled down from what it might have once been, the field had been sectioned off into smaller crops. Ben could see the remnants of corn and tomatoes. Lila pointed out a large section for potatoes. A massive hay field spread out beyond the fences.

They greeted the woman in charge, Gloria, whom they had met once in town. She was a husky woman of some indeterminate age who, they had learned, had grown up on farms. She offered to show them around.

"Most of the vegetables for the town are grown out here," she said. "We have large crops of corn and potatoes, because they are filling, and we have to take that into consideration. But we also grow lettuce, beans, kale, carrots, beets … you name it. And then we have hay for the animals.

"Who cuts it?" asked Lila.

"A few years ago we found a couple of antique harvesters that are pulled by horse, but most of it we do by hand. It's grueling work, but everyone in town chips in some time and we get it done."

"Not a lot of animals here," said Ben, looking around.

"Mostly chickens," said Gloria. "The town's egg supply comes from this farm. All of the other animals—the cattle, sheep, pigs, and the extra horses—are at the ranch."

"We're heading there next," said Lila.

They spent a little more time at the farm, but had seen all they needed to. They were anxious to continue their tour.

Back on the road, Lila asked Ben, "How are you doing? You're looking more comfortable."

"I like it," he answered. "Of course, maybe I just like the idea of not having to walk everywhere." He stroked Moose's mane. "But in all honesty, I think I'm feeling a connection. Moose seems to sense that I'm a new rider." He laughed. "I think he's taking it easy on me."

The wind began to pick up and black clouds appeared on the horizon.

"We'd better find some shelter," said Ben. "We probably have about ten minutes." Over the years he and Lila had become amazingly accurate in predicting how quickly a storm would be on them from the time they first saw the clouds.

"There's a house and barn," said Lila, pointing to a pair of structures about a half mile away.

They trotted up the road, slowly increasing speed as the horses sensed the coming storm. They reached the house as the first drops of rain began to fall. It was an abandoned property. The fields were in use for hay, most likely by the Monett people, but the house and barn hadn't seen any activity in years. The door to the barn had fallen off, so the trio, with Ralph following behind, rode the horses directly into the gloomy building just as the rain started in earnest. Lightning lit up the sky and thunder rumbled overhead.

They tied the horses to some beams and looked around, using flashlights to look into the darker corners. The barn had been home to many animals over the years, but none were there at that moment.

"Hey, look at this," said Lila, shining her light into a garbage can. She pulled out a faded McDonalds bag. "Blast from the past." They continued shining their lights and discovered a veritable treasure trove of artifacts from their old life in junk piles throughout the barn—broken TVs and computer monitors, a microwave, numerous lamps, and a washer and dryer.

"Kind of makes you wonder if society was more advanced before the event, or if maybe we're becoming more advanced now," observed Ben. "I know they all had their uses, but it just looks like crap now."

"What are all those things?" asked Katie, so they spent the next hour explaining what each thing did. Not ever having experienced electricity, they weren't sure how much of it all she comprehended.

By the time they finished, the storm had passed, and they were soon on their way again.

A few miles down the road, they saw the ranch. It was massive. Hundreds of cows and sheep were spread across the landscape, heads down and quietly chewing. The ranch itself was comprised of numerous buildings—a main house, a second building with several apartments, and three barns. Fenced off areas were full of pigs, goats, and other animals.

"Impressive," Ben said to Lila as they passed through the open gate into the ranch yard.

A black man a few years older than Ben was fixing a fence. He was of average height, but looked bigger. He was shirtless, displaying a muscular body. Ben was immediately struck by the size of the man's biceps.

"That guy's arms are thicker than my head," Ben said to Lila.

"I don't know," she replied with a laugh, "your head is pretty thick."

The man looked up from his work and saw his visitors. He peered at Ben and suddenly his face lit up in a smile. "Jordan," he called out. "You made it!" He put down his tools and walked out to greet them. "I wondered what had …" He stopped. His smile faded. "I'm sorry. I thought you were someone else."

Ben was confused. "I don't think I know you," he said, "But Jordan is my last name."

"No shit. You serious?"

"Yeah." Ben got off his horse and held out his hand. "Ben Jordan."

The big man shook his hand. Ben saw the initials USMC

tattooed down the man's forearm. "You're fucking kidding me," the man said. "Name's Rindell. You're really Ben Jordan?"

This couldn't be related to the Ben and Lila legend, thought Ben. Nobody knew his last name. In fact, Ben hadn't even uttered his last name in years. There was no reason to.

"You have me at a disadvantage," said Ben. "And I'm more than a little confused."

Lila and Katie had dismounted. "This is my wife, Lila, and my daughter Katie."

He shook Lila's hand. "Nice to meet you." He looked back at Ben. "I served with a guy at Pendleton named Jordan. Looked a lot like you. He'd be older though."

Ben's whole body shook. His legs suddenly couldn't hold his weight and he sat down in the dirt. When he spoke, it came out as little more than a whisper. "My brother was stationed at Camp Pendleton. Aaron Jordan. He was a sergeant."

"Yeah, that was him."

Ben tried to stand up, but his legs wouldn't work. Rindell reached down and helped him up. Ben leaned against the fence. Lila moved closer and took his hand.

"Between the event and the earthquake … figured San Diego was gone." Ben was trying to gather his thoughts.

"I'm sure it is," answered Rindell, a sadness in his voice. "I wasn't in San Diego though. I was in Yuma for some training. Your brother, too. We were down in the lower levels of a parking garage. A dozen of us. Had a day off from the training and were going to hang out in Yuma—what a fucking boring town that was." He looked at Katie. "Sorry."

Ben interrupted him. "Are you saying my brother might have survived the event?"

"I'm saying your brother did survive the event. All twelve of us did. We hung together for a while, but then split up. People wanted to check on their families. I came home to Missouri—hoping that someone would still be alive." His voice tailed off. Ben knew the meaning of that.

"Your brother and another guy named Bullock, they took off for somewhere in the northeast. Jordan said he knew his family was dead, but had to see for himself."

"My brother is alive?"

"We split up almost six years ago, but when I saw him last, yeah, he was definitely alive."

Ben sat down again on the ground. His legs felt like rubber.

"I ... I ..." He didn't know what to say. What could he say? He had just spent the last seven years assuming his brother had died in the apocalypse. His brain was a jumbled mess.

Lila jumped in. "Are you positive that the Jordan you knew is Ben's brother?"

"Can't be positive about nothin' anymore," replied the big man. "Just know that your boy here looks a lot like a guy I served with whose name was Jordan. Your brother a communications tech?"

Ben nodded dumbly.

Rindell shrugged, as if to say, There you have it.

Rindell saw the look on Ben's face and said, a little more softly, "Look, I got no doubt that the guy I served with was your brother. But I also know that a lot of shit has happened since then. He might be alive, he might be dead. Life and death is no big thing anymore. Either you're 'live or you're not. People alive one minute and dead the next. He coulda died the day after I saw him last. You just don't know. But let me tell you. He was a fuckin' Marine." He glanced down at Katie and shot Lila a look of apology. "If there's anybody who woulda survived, it was him."

He continued. "Want to hear something funny? Reason we were headin' for a bar in Yuma was that we just found out that day that we were deploying to Afghanistan in a coupla months. Don't think any of us even had a chance to call our families. We deployed alright. Straight to this shit wasteland."

Chapter 19

Six years earlier…

Aaron Jordan was nearing his destination. In a matter of days he would know the fate of his parents and younger brother. It had been a year since the catastrophe that ended most of the human life on the planet. He still didn't know the cause, and doubted he ever would, but he knew it wasn't just the States that had been hit. All the signs pointed to a worldwide event—no contact with anyone, no planes or helicopters from other countries … nothing. He had only been a Marine for about five years, but it was long enough. He could see the signs.

The first few months had been spent with his buddies trying to make sense of it all. At first they attempted to be of help to others, but there were so few others to help. Frustration and sorrow set in and they lapsed into a month-long drinking binge. When one of their group committed suicide in a drunken stupor, it seemed to sober up the others.

Then ones and twos they started to drift apart as the homeward tug took over. They all knew the answer to the obvious question—they knew their families were dead—but they had to prove it to themselves. What were their families doing when the end came?

Aaron and Sean Bullock set out together. It was a logical pairing for two reasons: One, they were best friends, and two, Sean was from Rhode Island, less than two hours by car from Aaron's home in Newton, Mass.

By the time they got on their way, the west coast earthquake and the Midwest earthquake had already hit. At the time, they had no idea that they were separate quakes, they just knew that every step of the way was a struggle. It took them months to get home. They stuck as best they could to the highways, but found themselves venturing far and wide to find walkable ground. Decomposition of the bodies had reached a bearable point, but it still sickened them to see the thousands of human remains every place they walked. As Marines, they were supposed to be tough—and they were—but this was too much. Their training had never prepared them for death of this magnitude.

Sean had grown up hunting with his father, so when they got tired of raiding supermarkets for cans of food—they had long since had their fill of C-Rations and MREs—Sean would shoot something fresh for dinner. Very quickly, Aaron translated his Marine Corps skills into hunting animals.

They ran into little trouble—not that there weren't some attempts by others to create problems for them, but that dissipated quickly. Although they no longer wore their uniforms—they had abandoned those many months before for the comfort of civilian clothes—there was no doubt in the eyes of any observer that they were military. One look at the way Aaron and Sean carried their M-16s was enough for potential troublemakers to give them a wide berth. Both men were expert marksmen, but luckily for most aggressors, they chose not to become the recipient of those skills.

Aaron didn't have to kill his first man until he was well into the trip east. They were somewhere in New York State— beyond the devastation caused by the earthquakes—when they ran across the girl.

She couldn't have been more than sixteen, and under different circumstances might have been pretty. But these weren't those circumstances. They were walking through what had once been an affluent suburban neighborhood and had rounded a corner made up of an eight-foot high fence. Not being able to see around the corner, they ran into the girl. Or rather, she ran into them—literally. She was a small girl, but was running hard and hit Sean with a force that knocked him over.

She didn't scream, but the fear in her face was beyond anything Aaron had ever seen. She pounced to her feet in an attempt to escape, but Sean held onto her.

"Whoa, whoa, whoa," he said.

"It's okay," said Aaron. "We're not going to hurt you."

Sean was an imposing presence at 6'2". Once over 200 pounds, the months of walking had slimmed him down. But the muscular upper body still complemented his height. He had also let his facial hair grow, giving him a sinister look. In fact, he was one of the nicest guys Aaron had ever met. Aaron, however, seemed more calming to her. At 5'10", clean-cut, and with an easy smile, he was able to gain her confidence fairly quickly.

"It's okay," Aaron repeated. "You don't have to be afraid of us. I'm Aaron, and this is Sean. We're U.S. Marines—well, we used to be." It was the first time Aaron had used that line since the world ended, but he felt it appropriate in this instance.

"What are you running from?" asked Sean.

"Them."

"And who are they?" asked Aaron patiently. He had a feeling it might take a bit to draw the story out of her. He was wrong.

"Ronald and James. We live in a big house with them. They make us do … things."

Aaron looked over at Sean. "I think we get the picture. Is it just Ronald and James?"

"And four women—me and Tiff and Sue and Roxy. They've had us there for a long time. I think maybe a year. Since a few weeks after … you know."

"How did you get out?"

"I was taking the garbage out and just ran. I couldn't go back." Tears were streaming down her face. "And because I ran, they're going to hurt my friends. That's what they always said. That's why we didn't run away before." She looked at them with a pleading expression. "Can you help them?"

Aaron and Sean looked at each other, thinking the same thing. Finally, a way for them to be of some use.

"Let's do it," announced Sean, getting to his feet.

"It's a few houses down," said the girl.

"Do they have weapons?" asked Aaron.

"A whole room full of them. They keep it locked. But they each have a gun in a holster on their belt." Her life suddenly looking less bleak, she was anxious to get back to the house. Now, instead of fear, Aaron could detect a feeling of payback emanating from her. He couldn't begin to imagine what the women had gone through over the last year.

It only took them a few minutes of walking until they came upon a large brick house—almost a mansion, thought Aaron—set back from the road. They heard voices as they approached. A man yelling and a woman screaming.

"Oh Brittany," a man called out in a sing-song voice. "We told you what would happen if you tried to run away. I know you can hear me. You show yourself or I'll slit Roxy's throat. She's the ugliest one here, so it'll be no loss. Get over here, Brittany!"

They now had a good view of the front yard. Standing at the edge of the driveway about 200 feet from them were two men—one in his forties or early fifties, and the other in his late twenties. The younger man was standing to the side watching the proceedings with a grin, while the older man had grabbed a woman by her hair and had pulled her head back, exposing her throat. In his hand was a large gleaming knife. The woman was close to the older man's age. She was screaming in pain and pleading for her life. Aaron could see the faces of two other women in the front window, crying.

"You've got to the count of ten," yelled the man. "One … two …" It was a slow count.

"I don't see us reasoning with them," said Sean.

"Me neither. You take out the young guy first. My guess is the older guy will probably let go of the woman in shock, giving me a clear shot."

"And if he doesn't?"

"Guess I'll find out how good I am."

Sean scrambled to a prone position, while Aaron kneeled against a rock. Both took aim.

"… eight … nine …"

Sean's M-16 let out two loud pops, and the younger man crumpled to the ground.

As expected, the older man's lower jaw dropped in shock. He looked around in panic and let go of the girl. Still holding the knife, he turned toward the house and Aaron put two rounds into his back. He ended up sprawled face-first by the front door.

Brittany left them and ran across the yard to her friend, who was lying on the grass gasping for air, fear having sapped the breath out of her. The other two women opened the front door and cautiously stepped over the dead man, looking at Aaron and Sean with a mixture of gratitude and fear.

While the four women were hugging, Aaron and Sean checked the two men, just to be sure. Then they sat on the grass and waited, just observing the situation. If Aaron had to guess, the chances were these women didn't know each other before falling victims to the now dead scumbags. It was clear, however that they were now fast friends—possibly the only family each would ever have again. Finally the women were calm, and the one called Roxy approached them.

"I don't know how I can thank you … how we can thank you."

"No need, ma'am," said Aaron. "Glad we could help. What do you plan to do now?"

"I have no idea."

"If I can make a suggestion?" The woman nodded. "We've seen a lot of the country. It's in pretty bad shape. I would urge you to find a settlement to join, but frankly, there don't seem to be too many of them. In some ways, you kind of have the best situation right here. If you've been here a year, then you made it through a winter—and if the weather was as bad here as it was in other places, that was an accomplishment." He looked at the roof. "Looks like those guys hooked up a woodstove."

"They did. It provides us with warmth and a place to cook."

"Then I suggest you keep this as your home. Without these guys, you can probably make a fair go of it."

The other women had crowded around.

"But we don't know how to defend ourselves in case people like them show up," said one of the others.

"Brittany said they had a roomful of weapons, right?" They nodded. "So we'll teach you to defend yourselves." He looked at Sean. "I suppose we can wait a few more days to get to our destination."

"I think you might be right."

Brittany and Roxy trusted the men from the beginning, but the other two held back, possibly fearing a repeat of what they had endured for so long. Aaron knew it was going to take a little while before they could gain a measure of their trust. They started by disposing of the bodies of Ronald and James. Then the women showed them the house. It was fairly comfortable, and once any remaining signs of Ronald and James were gone, Aaron was sure the women could make a go of it.

While the women purged the house of the frightening

memories, Aaron and Sean checked out the gun room. In fact, Ronald and James had acquired an impressive arsenal. It was obvious, however, that they knew very little about the weapons they had accumulated. Most of the guns were unloaded, and the ammunition was stacked in a corner in no particular order. If these men had needed to defend themselves quickly, it never would have happened.

They spent hours matching up ammo with weapon, labeling everything in the process. They wanted to make it as easy as possible for the women to be able to defend themselves. Tiffany and Sue remained the most timid, but it didn't stop Sue—the cook of the bunch—from preparing quite a meal from cans.

Ronald and James had kept an old, pre-computer chip, truck in the garage. The men used it to locate firewood to help the women make it through the winter. Certain things in the house had fallen into disrepair, and Aaron and Sean fixed what they could.

On the third day, they began the weapons training.

"Three things," said Aaron at the beginning of the training. "One: Never travel outside the perimeter of the yard alone. Always go in pairs when searching for food and other items. By the same token, always have two people in the house. No one should ever be alone. Two: Always carry a weapon when you are outside the house—not the yard, the house. The handgun on your hip should become part of you. When you leave the yard, also carry a rifle or a shotgun, whatever you become most comfortable with. Three: If you have to shoot at someone, shoot to kill."

"None of this shoot to wound bullshit you see in the

movies," interjected Sean. "If you're shooting at someone, you want to kill them. Pull the trigger twice. Try to put two bullets into them. It's called double tap. When you get good at it, you'll be able to put two bullets in a row in virtually the same spot."

"Also," added Aaron. "Keep practicing. Long after we're gone, you should have regular practice sessions. You have a shitload of ammunition, and we'll try to find more before we leave, so you should never run out."

"What about the noise?" asked Tiffany.

"Who's going to hear it?" asked Sean. "You're what's alive around here. And if someone does show up, better they know you're prepared for them."

They stayed two weeks. In that time, they all became good friends. The women began to pay attention to their appearance—not for Aaron and Sean's sake, as there was nothing sexual between them, but for themselves. They had spent so long trying to look unattractive so as to ward off the advances of Ronald and James, it was refreshing to them to suddenly have the confidence to care again.

The morning they left, the women were in tears. Aaron and Sean also had to fight back tears, and eventually lost the fight. They all hugged and Aaron promised if they headed back that way, they'd check in on them.

When they were out of sight, Sean turned to Aaron. "Hey."

"Yeah?"

"Remember in Yuma, we were all trying to find someone to help?"

"Yeah."

"Well it took almost a year, but we finally did some good."

"We did, didn't we."

Chapter 20

The next day, once they were out of the affluent suburb, they found what they were looking for—what would have done them no good in the earthquake-ravaged Midwest—an old vehicle that worked. It was a vintage Volkswagen Bug, hidden between two Lincoln Town Cars in the lot of an auto repair business. The tires were flat and the battery was dead, but with a little work, they got it running.

"Runs rough," said Sean when they finally got it started.

"Probably why it was at the repair shop," answered Aaron.

"Not very comfortable."

"You going to complain the whole way? Hey, if it gets us where we want to go, who cares."

"I do. What are you? 5'10"? 160 these days? You can fit that wimpy body into anything. Not me."

"I get your point. If we run across a Rolls Royce, we'll trade up."

"That's all I'm sayin'."

They still couldn't go fast, having to maneuver around the

thousands of cars stopped in the roads, but it beat walking. They made Rhode Island the next day. As they inched closer to Sean's home in Providence, Aaron noticed a change in his buddy. Sean didn't talk as much and spent a lot of time in space. Aaron wondered if he would be doing the same thing once they approached Newton.

They pulled up in front of what had once been Sean's house, a three-decker in an old neighborhood. Now it was a blackened hulk, as were all the houses around it.

Sean had tears running down his cheek.

"I'm sorry, man," said Aaron gently. He couldn't think of anything else to say.

They sat for almost half an hour without talking. Finally, Sean squeezed out of the car and walked over to his former home. Aaron climbed out and stood behind his friend.

"We lived on the first floor and rented out the other two. My cousin lived on the third floor. I lived here my whole life until I joined up."

"Maybe it's better this way. We've known our families are dead. Maybe the fire was good—like a cremation."

"Maybe." He was deep in thought again.

Aaron let him walk around the base of the structure, obviously reliving his memories. Finally Sean was done. He got out of it what he came for. The real mourning had taken place a year earlier for both of them. This was just a necessary tying up of a loose end. He walked over to Aaron with a trace of a smile on his face.

"Got a surprise for you." He strode to a covered car sitting at the curb in front of the house. "Never told you about this." He pulled back the cover, revealing a Ford Mustang convertible of an old vintage. "My dad's pride and joy. A '65 Mustang. If I can get it started, we can get rid of this shit box and drive something with class."

Aaron was excited too. Riding in the cramped VW was getting old already. Although it was fall, the weather—minus the routine violent storms—was still warm enough to enjoy driving with the top down.

Happy to move beyond the morbidity, he said, "Fucking fantastic. Let's do it."

It took them most of the rest of the day to clean it up and to find a bicycle pump to inflate the tires. Unbelievably, the battery still had a little life and the car started, albeit with much coaxing.

Finally, with whoops of joy at being in a real car again, they were on their way. Once again the going was slow, especially in downtown Providence. Sometimes they had to take several detours before being able to get to the roads they were looking for, but finally they landed on I-95 North and picked up speed. Sean drove in the breakdown lane some of the way, but in many places it had become overgrown from the grass on the side of the road. Almost three hours later they reached the outskirts of Newton, and Aaron directed Sean to his family's house.

As they were passing a shopping center, Aaron suddenly yelled out, "Pull in here."

Sean made a hair-raising turn into the parking lot and came to a stop. "Thanks for the warning," he said.

"No problem," answered Aaron, standing up and looking over the sea of cars.

"What are you looking for?"

"I think I saw my parents' car. Drive around closer to the supermarket."

In a minute they were stopped in front of a silver—or what used to be silver, now black from dirt—Subaru Outback.

"You sure this is it?"

"Look at the license plate."

The plate read "FNWAY."

"My brother Ben was a big Sox fan. When he saw this was available, he pleaded with my parents to get it."

He got out of the car and pulled out his Swiss Army knife and attempted to take the back plate off. Being plastic screws, they came out with ease.

"For old times," he said, and threw it in the backseat of the Mustang.

"If your car is here, it means..." started Sean.

"Yeah, I know. Probably my mom. She did the shopping." He hesitated. Finally he turned toward the supermarket. "I've gotta see," he said and slowly approached the door. Sean fired up the car and brought it up to the door.

"Don't want the car or our things out of my sight," he said.

Both men entered the store. Even though it was light outside, the inside was gloomy. They turned on flashlights. They carefully walked around the dead bodies, looking at each one, Aaron hoping he'd recognize something that belonged to his mother. By this time the bodies were nothing more than a little skin and hair, and the skeleton with some tattered clothes. They were able to look at them much more easily than during those weeks after the event when bodies were bloated and the smell and the flies were everywhere.

They searched for about fifteen minutes before Aaron

finally said, "I don't think she's here. Maybe she had to go into one of the other stores."

"There's one more over here," called out Sean, who had gone into the chip aisle to see if any of the cans of nuts were still good. "Someone put a tarp over her."

Sean had pulled the tarp partly off when Aaron got there. He gasped. All of a sudden he couldn't breathe. His heart was pounding so hard, he could feel it in his ears. He knelt down and looked at the form. "It's my mother. I'm sure of it." He had trouble getting the words out.

Sean picked up her bag and searched through for a wallet. He opened it to her driver's license, took it out, and handed it to Aaron. Aaron sat back against a shelf and let some tears come. Sean gave him his space. Finally Aaron rose. "Okay, I'm ready. Let's go." Now he was anxious to leave. There was nothing he could really do with the body. Burying it didn't make sense anymore. Besides, it wasn't his mother. It once was, but now it was no different than the thousands of other bodies they had walked over and around in the last year.

"You're serious, right?"

Aaron looked back at Sean. "What do you mean?"

"Man, you've gotten stupid over the last year."

"That's a given. I've stayed with you, right? That says it all."

"No, I'm serious. You don't see it?"

Suddenly Aaron did.

"Holy shit! How could I miss it?"

"I told you. 'Cuz you've gone stupid."

"Possibly." Aaron was deep in thought now. Finally, he said, "My mother couldn't have died under the tarp, so who put it over her?"

"And why her and no one else?" added Sean. "A family member or a friend?"

"A friend would be too busy dealing with their own dead family ..." Aaron left it hanging.

"Let's go to your house," suggested Sean.

They couldn't move fast enough. They hopped in the car, not even using the doors, and Aaron directed Sean to his house.

It was still there. The whole neighborhood was still there. All the yards had become overgrown, but the neighborhood was still recognizable. They pulled into the driveway. The house was as Aaron remembered it, just looking a bit weather-beaten. Two empty shopping carts from the same supermarket they just left were on their sides outside the front door. Aaron looked at them as he walked in the front door. Again, they had to use their flashlights. Immediately they saw the pile of food cans and other items in the middle of the living room. Some of the items had come from Eastern Mountain Sports near the supermarket. It was all survival gear of some sort.

"This came after," said Aaron.

Sean just nodded.

They walked into the kitchen. A few empty cans lined the counter, long since picked clean by the flies and worms and mice. Two dirty plates sat on the table, a candle between them. A roll of toilet paper was perched on the edge of the table.

"Someone was living here," said Sean. "Two people, if I had to guess."

"But not for very long," agreed Aaron. "A few days at most."

Aaron headed up the stairs, first checking his parents'

room, then Ben's. Nothing had been disturbed in his parents' room, but Ben's room looked like a tornado had hit it.

"Was it always this way?" asked Sean.

"Not this bad. I was the pig in the house, not Ben. He wasn't clean, but he wasn't this bad. Someone was looking for clothes. They're spread out all over the bed. Could it be a random person?" In his mind he was pretty sure not. Sean proved that theory a moment later.

"There's a picture frame on the bed, but the back has been taken off, and the picture is missing. Also, did your brother work at someplace called Maiden Farms Dairy? 'Cuz there's a shirt with a nametag on the floor."

"So he wasn't at work."

"Unless he had more than one nametag."

"From his description, I think they were too cheap for that. However, there's only one way to find out. Let's go to Maiden Farms Dairy."

Aaron gave Sean directions as they went, and they arrived five minutes later. It was starting to get dark outside, adding to the gloom inside the dairy. They walked through, shining lights on customers and employees alike. One man had his head down in a bowl. At this point, it had been reduced to some skin clinging to a skeleton, with a full head of hair. It was a hair-piece.

"Any other time," whispered Sean, pointing out the man to Aaron, "that would be funny. Not so much today." Being smaller than the supermarket, the restaurant had more of a tomb-like feel to it, and they felt the need to whisper.

There were only three male employees, two dead near the grill, and another outside an open walk-in freezer in the back room. Aaron checked outside, in case Ben had been on garbage duty.

He walked back in to the restaurant and said to Sean, "Ben's not here," with a little bit of hope in his voice.

"He was," replied Sean from the corner. He was standing in front of the time-clock. "He clocked in at 8:30am, and never clocked out. The clock reads 2:05, the time everything stopped. Aaron, it's looking like your brother may have survived this."

Chapter 21

"Holy crap, do you think he did, Sean?" asked Aaron, a bit shell shocked. All of the signs were leading to that assumption, but it was still a bit much to fathom.

"It looks that way, but don't get your hopes up. A lot of people survived who are dead now. Could he survive on his own?"

"Shit, no. I hate to say it, but my brother was pretty much of a wimp. I don't mean that as an insult. He just wouldn't have a clue of how to survive on his own."

"If that was him back at your house, it looks like he was with someone. Maybe that person knew what to do. Your dad, maybe?"

"Nothing in my parents' room was touched. No, it was someone else. Someone he met up with?"

"How about someone from here?" asked Sean. He got up and went to the time clock, sorting through the cards. "Nine people were working that day, including the manager. Let's match up nametags to the cards. It might give us a clue as to who he might be with."

They checked nametags and threw away the cards each time a match was made. Finally, they were left with two cards; Ben's and one other.

"Card says her name is Lila Martin," said Sean. "Date of birth ... oh shit. When this happened last year, she was only sixteen, a year younger than your brother."

"What's that old saying?" asked Aaron. "Something about babes in the woods?"

He felt deflated. Not only was Ben incapable of taking care of himself, if all this was true, he'd now also be responsible for a teenage girl. That couldn't be good.

They headed back to the house and settled down for the evening, eating from the pile of canned and freeze-dried food left in the living room.

"So what do we do now?" asked Sean.

"Wish I had a clue as to where they went."

"Aaron, look," began Sean. "The fact that your brother might have been alive a year ago is great—no, it's fantastic. But this is a big country and we have no way to know where they went. It's not like they caught a bus and we can track them down. Hell, there's not even anyone to ask. Look at it this way: The fact that they didn't stay here and curl up into a little ball is a positive sign. They made a move. They did something. They were collecting food for a journey, so they had someplace in mind, probably. You have to have faith that just maybe they survived. Stranger things have happened."

"I want to believe that he made it, but it's hard, 'cuz I knew him. This would have overwhelmed him."

"Everyone is capable of reaching deep down and coming

up with something that will take them a step further. You gotta have faith."

"You're right. I have to believe he's still alive."

"Here's the thing. We've got to get on with our lives. All we can do is move on. If we see other people, we can ask if they've seen him. Maybe someday we'll hear something. Consider this a victory. You came here expecting to find your family dead, but there is a chance that your brother is still alive. That's one hell of a victory."

"Okay, then. Suggestions on where to head?"

"I liked Cali, but I'm sure that's gone. Hell, Aaron, I'll be honest. I always hated living in the East. Yuma mighta sucked, but I liked it out West. If it wasn't for the way the earthquakes fucked up everything, I could head out there. Mainly I want to get out of here. We saw what we came for. Now let's get the fuck out."

"Can't disagree with you. How about Florida? Soak up some sun on the beaches. It's not West, but it's a long way from here."

"Let's do it. Leave in the a.m.?"

"Sounds good. How about we take a detour and stop by and see the women, then go south from there?"

They were on the road bright and early, and the next day were driving down the suburban street in Western New York about a mile from their destination.

And then the earthquake hit. The last of the three. The final screw in the total devastation of the United States. It hit fast and hard. One minute they were enjoying the sun on their faces and the wind in their hair, and the next a gaping hole opened up in front of them, partially swallowing the car. Sean smacked his head against the steering wheel and Aaron sailed over the windshield and landed on the hood of the car. Since the car was at an angle in the hole, he rolled down the hood and landed hard on the pavement.

The ground was still shaking, and Aaron observed houses on both sides of the street collapsing in on themselves. Finally, it stopped and Aaron unsteadily picked himself up off the ground. Nothing was broken, just some scrapes. He quickly checked on Sean, who was moaning. He pulled him out of the car and set him down on some grass, then retrieved their backpacks and guns. By the time he got back to his friend, he was sitting up holding his head.

"What the fuck! Look at my car!"

Aaron pulled some antiseptic and a bandage from one of the backpacks. As he was applying the antiseptic, Sean yelled, "Ow! Shit, that hurts."

"Shut up you weenie and let me do my job."

"Bite me."

In five minutes, Sean was standing up with a white bandage wrapped around his head. "We need to check on the girls."

They double-timed it down the road and reached the yard in a few minutes. The house was a pile of rubble. Something inside—probably the woodstove—had started a fire, and the flames were reaching into the sky. They quickly determined that whoever had been in the house had probably been killed by the quake. If not, the fire would have consumed them.

And then they saw her. Looking as pitiful as the day she had run into Sean was Brittany, sitting alone on the grass, her head in her hands.

"Brittany!" called out Sean.

She looked up in surprise and burst into tears when she saw them. She got to her feet and ran to them, almost unseeing through her tears, and latched herself to Sean.

Aaron called out over the roar of the inferno that was the house, "Brittany, are the others in there?"

She nodded her head weakly and sank further into Sean's arms.

Hours later, Brittany was able to talk about it. Aaron and Sean had set up a tent on the front lawn, the smoldering house serving as extra warmth on a night that had turned chilly. Aaron was cooking some beef stew while Sean sat with Brittany.

She was in the outhouse in the backyard when the quake hit. The flimsy building disintegrated around her and she was thrown to the grass. The back of the main house had already collapsed, so she ran around to the front, arriving in time to see the whole house implode.

"I could hear them screaming," she said in a monotone. "I wanted to help them, but I couldn't. Then the screaming stopped. Right after that, the fire started. It just all happened ... so fast."

She fell asleep a few minutes later.

"Well that changes things," said Aaron, after she had fallen asleep clutching Sean's leg for comfort.

"Gotta bring her with us."

"Of course. Just thinking about the quake. One that size would've affected things halfway down the east coast ..."

"And you're thinking it's not going to be any easier heading south than it would be to go west," interrupted Sean.

"Something like that."

"More cities to try to wade through, too."

"I like the wide open spaces out west," said Aaron.

"Why are we even bothering to discuss it? I think we've both made up our minds. West it is."

They packed up the next day. Sean continued to bemoan the loss of his car. Aaron knew the convenience and fun of the car was only part of the story. It was just another memory from Sean's earlier life that was now gone. But they both knew from their trip east that a car was useless now in the fractured landscape. They'd be hoofing it once again. They found a backpack for Brittany at a local sporting goods store and filled it with clothes and toiletries. They tried to make it as light as possible, but it was still heavy. They knew that, over time, her body strength would increase and wearing it would become second nature.

Brittany proved hardier and more resilient than the two men expected. The first three days on the road, they made a lot of time with nary a complaint from the girl. Aaron couldn't help noticing her attachment to Sean, rarely leaving his side. He had become her protector, her brother, her father, and—he had a sneaking suspicion—someday her lover. He didn't see Sean spurning her attachment, and he seemed to be reveling in it to some extent. The world had changed, thought Aaron. What had once been acceptable—or not acceptable—in society was moot now. You took love where you could find it. Moments of enjoyment and happiness were few and far between.

Their journey was uneventful. They saw small groups of people, but no established settlements. Aaron made sure to ask each group they ran across if they had heard of his brother, but to no avail. Everyone was yearning for some missing or dead loved one, so to be asked about yet another one was given little importance.

A month into the trip—somewhere in Ohio—they came across a larger group. At almost a hundred people, it was nearly a town. However, that was where the resemblance ended. They had taken over a trailer park near the shores of a lake. The people weren't doing well, though. They had food and shelter, but little more. It was what they didn't have that was so obvious. They had no spirit. It broke Aaron's heart to see so much misery in the group. Especially the children.

They were greeted with little enthusiasm and the three were just going to pass through quickly, but Aaron felt he should ask the question anyway. They were talking to a small group of the residents and Aaron asked if any had ever run across a Ben Jordan. They looked at him blankly.

Then one of the men said, "Don't know anyone's last name anymore. The only Ben I've heard of was the half of the couple, Ben and Lila."

Aaron looked at Sean. "Yeah," he responded. "He was with a girl name Lila. You saw them?"

"Hell, no. But I've heard the stories. Everyone's heard the stories."

"What stories?" Aaron wanted to shake the guy to get him to talk faster.

"This couple, Ben and Lila, helped a bunch of people. Lotta bad folks out there. Rumor is they killed a lot of them. A dozen or more."

"Hell Sam," blurted out another man, "way more than that. Three or four dozen's what I heard."

"You're kidding." Aaron looked at Sean in amazement. "My brother?" He turned back to Sam. "Do you know where they are now?"

"Disappeared, is what I heard. There one minute, gone the next. Maybe dead. Don't know. Some people say they're angels from heaven. Fucking idiots. No angels on this piece of shit earth."

They talked for a while longer, but got nowhere, so they thanked him for the information and were on their way.

"Should we go look for him?" Aaron asked that night when they had set up camp. Brittany had already fallen asleep. He answered his own question. "Yeah, I know. Stupid thought. If they are alive, they could be anywhere. Can you believe that? My brother?"

"We don't know how much of it is true, but it's got to be based on something," said Sean. "I say we keep going. This country has become very small. Somewhere down the line some more information might come our way. Let's deal with it then."

*****

They finally holed up for the winter in a house someplace in Iowa. Like the house Brittany had lived in, it was set up with a wood stove and would provide them with a safe and warm place away from the elements. They stocked it up with massive amounts of canned food from a supermarket that hadn't been too badly looted, as well as stacks of books raided from the local library. They each had a bedroom, but within a month of moving in, Brittany no longer stayed in hers, preferring instead to bunk with Sean. Aaron understood and didn't begrudge his friend his chance at female companionship.

For him though, it was going to be a long winter.

*****

And it was. It was a hard winter weather-wise. Blizzard after blizzard piled the snow to the point where leaving the house became almost impossible. They cleared a path to their makeshift toilet, an area that started out as a ditch that they would cover with dirt. But once the snow came and piled on it, they just kept an area as clear as possible and did their business on top, shoveling it away as it froze. They also had a path to the detached garage, where they stored their wood.

Other than the weather, it was an easy winter; lots of reading and game-playing. Aaron was lonely for female companionship, and seeing that, Brittany—after talking to Sean—offered to sleep with him once a week or so. While he appreciated—and was tempted by—the offer, he declined. Somehow, it felt like pity-sex. And besides, Sean and Brittany had a real thing going. The last thing Aaron wanted to do was screw up their relationship or his friendship with Sean.

Finally spring came, and brought with it an early heat-wave, allowing them to finally leave their winter prison by early April.

By mid-June, having maneuvered around countless ravines caused by the earthquake, they found themselves in the rolling hills of western Nebraska. They still hadn't really decided on a destination, but there was something freeing about the journey, so they had pretty much decided to keep heading west until they reached the ocean.

It had just gotten dark, and they were building a fire at their campsite among the rocks, when Brittany exclaimed, "Hey, what's that?" She pointed to a gap in the hills.

Aaron and Sean had also just seen it.

"Fire?" asked Sean.

"I don't think so," answered Aaron. "It's different somehow."

"Man made," said Brittany. "You know, like streetlights or lights from buildings."

"Holy shit, you're right," said Aaron. "Could it be that someone has figured out how to get the power back?"

It was too late to investigate that night, but early the next morning they were on their way, full of anticipation. Late in the afternoon they came over a rise and were presented with the source of the lights. Far to their left and right were the remains of a small city, mostly burned and obviously abandoned. In front of them, though, on the banks of a river, was a much smaller town, newly built. It only consisted of a few dozen houses and trailers and some buildings that comprised a makeshift downtown. Next to the town, on the edge of the river, was a small power plant with smoke rising from a smokestack. The town had power!

An hour later they walked down the main street. They hadn't seen any vehicles, but the buildings definitely had lights. It wasn't heavily populated. Based on the number of houses, Aaron figured it couldn't have a population much more than a hundred. However, people were milling around, talking and laughing—such a far cry from the trailer park they had run across in the fall.

A man approached them from one of the buildings and held out his hand.

"I'm Joe Baxter," he said with a wide smile. "I'm the mayor—such as the office is—and official greeter. It's always nice to see new people walk into town."

He swept his arm around to indicate the town, and said, "Welcome to Paradise."

Chapter 22

This was all too much. My brother might be alive? It had now been over seven years since civilization had disappeared, and almost eight since I last saw Aaron. I felt guilty. I missed my family big time for a few months after the event, until our life got so complicated my family was pushed to the background. Over the years though, I thought of my parents on a regular basis. The memory of Aaron, however, had begun to fade long ago. He was six years older than me and hung with a whole different crowd. Somehow though, he always found time for me. And maybe that's why I was feeling guilty. He was a good brother. Shouldn't I have spent more time missing him?

There was precious little information Rindell could give them about Aaron that would be of any help, so he took them on a tour of the ranch. Ben barely heard or saw anything. The only other time he had ever been this stunned was when Lila informed him that she was pregnant with Katie.

They stayed about an hour. It was mid-afternoon and they wanted to get back before dark, so they said their goodbyes and started on their way. Ben was quiet for much of the ride home, still trying to process the information.

"Daddy, why are you so quiet?" asked the ever-observant Katie.

Ben didn't know what to say, so Lila jumped in and explained it to Katie as best she could. She finished with, "So Daddy hasn't seen his brother in a long, long time and he misses him a lot. Maybe he'll be able to see him again someday."

They arrived back at the stable as the sun was starting to set, and it was dark when they got back to the house. Ben lit the stove and the kerosene lanterns while Lila gave Katie a bath and got her ready for bed.

"Do you think he's still alive?" Ben asked Lila when they were in bed and Katie was long-since asleep.

"If he really did survive the initial event, I'd say there's a good chance of it. After all, he had skills that most people didn't—certainly a lot more than we had. On the other hand, I don't want you to get your hopes up."

"That ship has sailed. Until I find him, or find out that he's dead, I think I'm going to always be looking. Wherever we go, I'll always be studying faces and asking people if they've seen him. How could I not do that? He's my brother."

*****

Over the next month Ben joined with other residents to make trips by wagon to Springfield and to the Joplin area in search of canned goods and other supplies. Although both towns had been picked over, mostly by the Monett residents on previous trips, they still found stores that had been untouched. When he wasn't on scavenger hunts, he was chopping wood or hunting—with Katie when she wasn't in school. It left him little time to think about finding his brother or traveling to Yellowstone. Lila was working just as hard smoking meat and fish for the long winter ahead and getting the house prepared. She tried chopping wood, but her lack of vision on one side threw off her aim. Finally she gave up and left it to Ben.

As busy as they were though, they knew that, come spring, they'd be back on the road. The Monett community was pleasant, but it wasn't for them.

When winter arrived, it came with a vengeance. Luckily, their years in the forest had given them the know-how to prepare for it. But as ready as they were, the sheer ferocity still managed to catch them by surprise. Every week brought at least one snowstorm—oftentimes there were multiple storms. With the snow came the wind. While the streets remained almost free of the snow as the wind whipped across the plains, the buildings had many feet of drifts running up their sides. While Ben was constantly shoveling out his doors, some residents never saw their front doors all winter if their houses were faced toward the constant oncoming wind. They used back doors—and sometimes even windows—to go in and out.

Katie moped most of the winter. There was no way to get to the stables to spend time with Scooby. Her horse had become her best friend, and she missed him dearly.

Early one morning about mid-winter, Ben and Lila were awakened by a frantic knocking at their front door. Their neighbor Mary was screaming that her roof had fallen in and Ellis, her husband of almost forty years, was inside. The snow had gotten too heavy in the section of roof over their living room. The residents came out in force to clear away the snow and debris. It took several hours, but they eventually reached her husband, who had been crushed to death by a beam.

Another neighbor took in the distraught Mary. A week later, the heartbroken widow slipped out in the middle of the night during another round of snow and wind, and disappeared into the storm. They all looked for her the next day, but with the knowledge that they wouldn't find her alive. In fact, they never found her body at all.

"This isn't the first time I've seen that happen," said Brian later that day over a cup of coffee at Ben and Lila's home. "Two winters ago, it happened twice." He took a sip, then continued. "Surviving the event was one thing—sheer luck for all of us. Living through the hardships and dangers that followed was a major accomplishment. There probably isn't one person alive today who didn't come close to death more than once in the last seven years. Despite all that, what have we really achieved? Life is still hard and it will always be hard. We just approach it with varying degrees of contentment—I hesitate to use the word happiness. I'm doing okay and you guys look like you're fine. But not everyone is fine. There are some who wake up every morning wondering why they even bother to go on. And then it finally hits them—they really don't want to go on. Wandering away, especially in the bitter cold where you can lie down and just never wake up, seems the least violent way to call it quits. The only thing keeping Mary and Ellis going was each other. With Ellis gone, this became an even uglier world for Mary."

"And maybe that's why the Nebraska town appeals to

some," put in Lila. "Just the thought of electricity gives people a little hope."

"No matter how much they hope for it," said Ben, "the world will never be like it was. Some random electricity won't change that."

There wasn't much to say after that and Brian soon left.

"Are you happy?" asked Lila, once Brian was gone.

"I am. I have you and Katie."

"Putting us aside for a minute, are you happy?"

"It's impossible to put the two of you aside, but I know what you're asking. Do I wish the world was the way it used to be? Sometimes. Sometimes it's so exhausting to just survive that I think back to a time when life was easy. Baseball, movies, music … you name it. But I only think like that in times of exhaustion. In other ways, I'm living life in a way that would have been unthinkable to me before all this happened. And I truly believe the world has been given a do-over. It might take centuries for some sort of global society to emerge, but it will. We have so many books of history that future generations can learn from—books that our ancestors didn't have."

He thought for a minute.

"But then, it comes back to you and Katie. It's the two of you who make me happy, and I can't separate you from everything else. And now I'll ask you the same thing: Are you happy?"

"I am. Like you, it's the three of us together that makes me happy. Oddly enough, I don't miss our old world. I wasn't particularly comfortable in it. It wasn't just my disinterested parents, it was everything. I felt like a visitor, not a participant. When this all happened I felt somehow free. It's been a struggle, certainly, but I still feel free." She touched her eye patch. "I wish that hadn't happened. If it wasn't for you and Katie, I might have been like Mary and just taken that last walk. I guess I felt it took away some of my freedom—and it did to an extent. But I'm over that now. I look forward to the rest of my life and the challenges in store." She lowered her voice. "Once we get out of here. I'm anxious to see what Yellowstone holds."

That night they made love for hours, their earlier conversation sparking a deep desire for the physical closeness that was sometimes forgotten in the sheer enormity of work they each had on a daily basis, and that caused them to be exhausted by nightfall.

About mid-March, based on a lunar chart Brian had found, the snow stopped. As had happened before, it was a sudden shift from winter to spring. The wind direction shifted and warm air began to flow in, slowly melting the mountains of snow. That caused a sudden onset of flood season, creating a different set of problems.

Ben and Lila were itching to get on the move, despite Brian's attempts to convince them to stay. In the end, he understood. The rules of the new world had changed, or more accurately, there were no rules, and everyone had to find the place that would bring them the greatest amount of comfort. It was obvious from the beginning that Monett wasn't the place for Ben and Lila.

The goodbyes were tearful, but finally they were on their way. The plains were very different from much of their trip to Monett. It was a strange combination of the wild and unfamiliar mixed with their childhood images of the plains. Where the ground wasn't cracked, nothing had changed other than roads being overgrown. There were miles and miles of gently waving grasses and grains. But where the cracks appeared, wild growth emanated, sometimes soaring twenty feet into the air. However, with the horses, finding the ending point of a crevasse was accomplished a lot quicker. Working their way around a particularly large ravine could now take hours instead of days.

Cities and towns were further apart, but they were amazed at the few they did run across. The weather had taken an even greater toll on them than it had on the towns to the east. Those that weren't burned were beginning to crumble, caused in part by the rapid growth of the plants, and in part by the extremes in the weather.

"I think the transformation of the landscape is going to happen a lot sooner than we thought," said Lila, as they looked out at a particularly devastated town.

"I'm glad," responded Ben. "The sooner the old world is gone, the better for everyone, I think."

They tried to keep their days in the saddle fairly short, mostly for Katie's benefit. Despite her riding expertise, she was still just a little girl. Although the lack of an accurate calendar kept them from pinpointing her birthday, they figured she was rapidly approaching her seventh birthday. At seven—even in the new world—rest was required. In truth, Ben and Lila appreciated the stops as well. They were coping well with the transition to horseback, but it was still a relatively recent addition in their life.

It was late spring when they rounded a bend and saw the sign that they had been waiting for:

Yellowstone National Park.

Chapter 23

They got off their horses and hugged. Even Ralph wanted to be part of the celebration, although he had little idea why. Lila walked over to the sign and hugged it as well.

Under the Yellowstone National Park sign was a second sign, a crude board with the words Rock Creek Settlement, approx. 20 miles painted in black. There was an arrow pointing up the dirt road. As they had run across many times in their travels, the road had most likely once been concrete, and somewhere under the many layers of dirt and rock it likely still was.

"It really exists," said Lila quietly, almost in relief. She took out a small towel from her saddlebag and wiped the sweat from her face. She took off the patch and carefully dried it, then wiped around her damaged eye. She put the patch back in place, looked at her husband and daughter, and said, "Are we ready?"

"We are," answered Ben.

"Then let's go," said Katie, anxious to meet some more

children her age.

Ben noted to himself that she had long since graduated from her shyness.

They took their time. They had made it this far. There was no reason to rush the last twenty miles. They walked the horses, Ralph—as was his habit—sometimes sauntered behind, sometimes ahead of the group, and at times would take off for a little while and explore.

Once, they smelled wood smoke, and knew that a home was somewhere nearby. A mile or so beyond that they passed a house that had been built within view of the road. There was no one to be seen, but it was a lived-in house with a huge garden being prepared for the summer season.

I found it interesting the living situations that brought people comfort. Just based on the two hints of civilization we had run across in Yellowstone so far—the wood smoke house and the home we were now passing—people had very different ways of adapting to the new world. The wood smoke people obviously wanted complete privacy, because their home was nowhere to be seen. The people living in the one we were passing were most likely more social, wanting the occasional company of other humans. We were definitely more like the former, and would seek out some private spot off the beaten path.

They rode into Rock Creek in the late afternoon. The relief Ben and Lila each felt was palpable. It was the realization that the journey they started ten months earlier—by Ben's calculations—was finally over. But there was also the relief that the fabled settlement in Yellowstone really did exist.

The town itself was small, but Ben noticed a fair amount of new construction going on. They had heard that most of the residents of the settlement lived in the hills, but it was clear that the town itself was attracting people as well.

The hard-packed dirt main street consisted of a small school, a larger building that housed the church and community center, a building with a handmade sign that read Town Exchange, a doctor's office, veterinarian's office, a dentist, a barber/hairdresser, and a blacksmith. There was even a small restaurant. Other buildings were under construction along the main street, but most of the building activity were houses on the outskirts.

"Does this bring you back to stories of the old west?" asked Lila. "I mean, a blacksmith?"

"I guess now that horses and plows are back in style, someone needs to take care of the shoeing and fixing the equipment. I'm just wondering how people get paid for their services. Bartering, I suppose?"

The Town Exchange seemed to be the busiest place, so they pulled up. There was actually a hitching post in front of the store. They dismounted and tied their horses to the post. Ben helped Katie off her horse and they all stretched. They had been on horses for a long time and it took a moment to regain their footing.

"I'll forever be bow-legged," said Lila, looking down.

Their appearance had roused interest among the townspeople, several of whom came over to welcome them.

"Thank you," said Ben, in response. "We've been riding a long time, and we didn't know if the town even really existed.

It was mostly rumor up until now. Who would we talk to about settling here?"

"Best bet is in The Exchange," answered a white-haired man with a slight stoop. "Not sure who's in there right now, but they can direct you. Welcome again."

"Thanks so much," said Lila. Ben noticed that she hadn't stopped smiling from the moment they arrived.

They walked into the store and were struck by the size of the building, much larger than it appeared from the front. Every conceivable nook and cranny was crammed with useful items—knives, shovels, canned goods, kitchen utensils, paint ... the list went on. It seemed like a mini department store. Four people were wandering the aisles picking out items and placing them in baskets. Behind the counter was a bear of a man—tall and clean-cut, but imposing. He had a smile on his face and held out his hand. "Sean."

Ben shook his hand. "I'm Ben, this is my wife Lila, and our daughter Katie."

The man's eyes grew wide. "Holy shit!" he exclaimed. He looked at Katie. "Sorry."

"That's okay. I know that word."

Ben, of course, assumed it was related to the stories about them, so his head spun when the man uttered his next words.

"Ben Jordan, nice to finally meet you. Do you know that you didn't clean up your dinner dishes when you left your house almost eight years ago?"

Ben was at a loss. All he managed was a "huh?"

Sean burst out laughing. "Believe it or not, I was in your house in Newton."

Ben looked at Lila, thoroughly confused.

"Let me explain."

Lila's left eye crinkled as a smile spread across her face. "Please do," she said, her interest now piqued.

"Rumor was that you might be dead, but your brother didn't believe it. Knew he'd run across you someday."

"My brother is here?"

Sean's face clouded over. "No. I wish he was though. Long story. Let me close up here and you can come to my house. I'll explain it all then."

He waited for the browsers to finish. Meanwhile, Ben and Lila walked around the shop. It was a microcosm of the world they left behind—everything from books to knickknacks, food, clothes, gadgets, even drugstore reading glasses.

Lila held up an antique meat grinder, just like the one they had to leave behind at Fontana Lake. "Ben, look," she said.

"Just like home," he answered.

The only thing missing was anything electronic. Ben was amazed at how much Sean had crammed into his shop.

"Where did you get all this?" he asked.

"Forays into towns. Not so easy anymore. So many towns were destroyed by the earthquake or by fire that any place still standing has long since been cleaned out. So my trips have become a lot longer as I have to travel further."

"Why?" asked Ben. "I guess I mean why do you do it?"

"Why do I have a business when there's no longer any money?"

Ben nodded.

"We still have a society. We all have an obligation to help others. We have a doctor, a vet, a teacher, a minister. Hell, we even have a lawyer to help mediate disputes. If I hurt myself, I go to the doctor. He might not have the drugs he once had, but he's still a doctor. He still has the skills. He can do more than I can. Same goes for things. People need things, but not everyone can get them themselves. Not everyone can go far and wide to collect the items they need. That's where I come in. I can do that when others can't."

Only two shoppers were left in the store, and they were aware that Sean wanted to close up, so they were hurrying.

"Look," Sean continued. "All we have is each other. The world is very different from the one we used to have. People recognize that we've gotta help each other. It's the only way we'll survive and have something to give our kids."

Lila joined them.

Sean said, "You guys should know that better than anyone. If the rumors are true, you were instrumental that first year in keeping people's hopes alive."

"So is everything based on bartering?" asked Lila.

"Pretty much. We're always refining the system, but yeah. We all have skills that somebody can benefit from, even if it's as simple as trading a meal for a dentist visit. It's still pretty loose. If somebody wants something from the store, they can take it. They'll find a way to repay me for it. You know what's cool?" he asked. "People aren't greedy. They don't take things they don't need. People value things now. It's refreshing."

"It's amazing that everyone embraces it," said Lila.

"Not everyone has," he answered. "And if they can't, they are asked to leave. We have very few rules here, but they are all different ways of saying the same thing: 'You live in harmony with your community, or you are not welcome here.' Surprisingly, those who can't follow that rule are usually happy to leave."

Clearly, society was starting over. But I had to wonder how long bartering was going to last as a form of payment. And yet, what else would work? Money was worthless. Gold, the monetary standard for centuries, was simply a shiny rock. What could take the place of bartering? What could possibly have value anymore? Sheep, goats, and pigs? Bottle caps? I had no idea. If it continued to be successful, bartering seemed the only option. And I couldn't foresee it changing for many years—maybe even well beyond my lifetime.

The store was empty, so Sean put up a sign in the door that read: Closed. But if you need anything, help yourself. Just close the door after you. Thanks!

Ben and Lila looked at each other and just smiled.

Sean had one of the homes close to town, so they walked their horses, with Ralph running behind. They were silent as they walked, Ben and Lila taking in the feel of the town and Sean being aware enough to let them.

Though it was small, it had potential, thought Ben. What would it look like in ten years? Certainly there would be more building. Not everyone who had survived that long would want to live away from the center of action. While he and Lila weren't alone in their need to be away from civilization, it was just human nature to want to congregate in a group. No, Rock Creek would someday be a bustling community with a strong core, and it would be people like Sean who would lead it.

But it came with so many questions: Would there be

power? Even if other towns—like the Nebraska people—had power, Rock Creek was so remote that he wasn't so sure they would ever get it. He didn't know if that would hurt or help the future of the town. People were used to living without power, and as he saw in Monett, many now seemed to prefer it.

Another question was commerce. Would they continue to live in a barter society? Would some sort of money appear. Ben had trouble imagining bartering on a large scale. Would the greed that had formed much of his old world return?

All questions for another day. For now, they needed to build a life in Yellowstone … and he needed to learn about his brother.

They arrived at a large, but simple house. On the farmer's porch along the front wall sat a young woman about Lila's age with two children playing at her feet.

Ben and Lila tied their horses to the porch and Sean made the introductions.

"Honey, this is Ben, Lila, and Katie. This is my wife, Brittany and our children, Tiffany and Aaron. Tiff is three and Aaron is one."

"Ben and Lila?" asked Brittany.

"The same," answered Sean. "Alive and kicking."

Brittany got up and gave them hugs. "You look like your brother," she said to Ben.

"C'mon in," said Sean. "I know you're anxious to hear about Aaron, so we have a lot to talk about."

Chapter 24

The inside of the house was decorated in a western motif, as befitting the location. It had two bedrooms, a kitchen with a cast-iron cook stove, and a comfortable living room with a large woodstove in one corner.

"You must be thirsty," said Brittany. "I'll get you some water. I'll also put some tea and coffee on."

"Thank you," replied Lila. She felt an immediate kinship with Brittany. Maybe it was their closeness in age, or maybe because Lila sensed that they had shared similar experiences.

"Have a seat," offered Sean. Katie wandered over to a corner where Tiff and Aaron were playing. She sat down with them and observed, occasionally picking up unfamiliar toys.

"The last I knew," began Sean, "your brother was living in Paradise."

"Paradise?" asked Ben.

"A town in Nebraska that has power."

"The evil," said Lila quietly.

Sean cocked his head. "The evil?"

Ben and Lila took turns telling the stories they'd heard about the town, and Lila gave her first-hand account of the skirmish in Monett.

Sean looked at Brittany. Her eyes were wide.

"Things had gone downhill when we were there, but we left more than three years ago. Things had become ominous at that point, but it blows me away to think that's what it has become. I'll be honest with you. It makes me a little worried about your brother, because there is no way he would put up with that shit."

Ben felt his heart drop into his stomach.

"It wasn't always evil, though," said Sean. "In the beginning, 'Paradise' was an appropriate name for it."

"What changed?"

"What always changes things for the worse? Greed." He was silent, seemingly reflecting on the last few years. Finally he spoke. "But let me tell you a little bit about your brother first."

He began with Yuma and told them the story of heading east to Rhode Island and Massachusetts, and of finding clues as to the possible survival of Ben.

"We wondered who covered your mother in the supermarket, and ..."

"You saw my mother?"

"Yes ... sorry," answered Sean, suddenly realizing the sensitivity of the situation. He moved on quickly, describing the visit to the house and the restaurant. "There were clues that you may have survived, but Aaron didn't want to have too much hope. But I knew deep down that he wanted to believe it. Although," he chuckled, "he was pretty sure you were too inept to survive."

Ben smiled. "I was." He looked at Lila. "We both were. Somehow we made it through."

"Somehow? Not the stories I heard. Anyway," he went on to relate their adventures heading west, meeting Brittany, and finally showing up in Paradise.

"So, it was different back then?" asked Ben.

"Totally. It was the early days of Paradise. It had promise … so much promise."

Brittany brought tea and homemade cookies and sat down next to Sean.

"How much power did the town have?" asked Lila.

"Not much at first. When we got there, it had lights. They were dim, but they worked. You have to understand, it wasn't like now, where we've been used to living with no power for so long. We still missed the conveniences back then. Even a little bit of electricity was intoxicating." He took a sip of his tea and put his hand over Brittany's.

"Was it an established town or a new one?" asked Ben.

"Kind of a cross between the two. There was a town—or the remains of one—nearby, but it wasn't inhabited. This town sprang up in the parking lot of a small power plant on the banks of a river. Over time it expanded beyond the parking lot. That's when we arrived. We were met by a man named Baxter. He had been an engineer at the plant when the power went out. He spent a year trying to get the power back, and eventually succeeded to some degree. By then, a couple dozen people had congregated around the plant in tents, and a small community popped up. Baxter was a really good guy whose singular purpose was to bring power back to the country as best he could. His strength, however, was also his weakness. He was a nuts and bolts engineer, not a leader. Smart and cordial, but his vision was focused in on the power, not building a town. By the time we got there, a town council was in place."

"The beginning of the end," said Brittany in a quiet voice.

"It was," agreed Sean. "Problem was, we didn't see it until it was too late. I suppose it was the beginning of the 'evil', as you call it, but it was enough for us, so we left."

"And my brother?"

"He chose to stay. He really had no choice. It was the age old story. He had fallen in love. Emily was the only teacher in the town and wouldn't leave her kids. No matter how bad it got, she felt she couldn't leave them without a teacher."

"And Aaron couldn't leave Emily," added Brittany. "We understood. When love hits, you can't really do anything about it. She felt she had a job to do, and Aaron decided his job was to protect her and make sure she had the freedom to teach."

"And no matter how bad it got," said Sean, "Aaron was the one person they didn't mess with in that town, so Emily had free reign at the school."

"Why wouldn't she?" asked Lila.

"Well, that brings us back to the story of the town. I imagine in your travels you've run across a fair amount of greed and power trips."

Ben and Lila glanced at each other, and the memories rushed in—the camp where Lila had been held prisoner; Ben's long months in the prison cell in Washington. Those were the extremes, but how many other examples had they encountered that were just as insidious, but not as overt and organized?

"We've seen our share," answered Ben.

"Well, it was no different in Paradise. The town council

was full of people who all 'knew'"—he made quotation marks with his fingers—"the right way to do things. With such a small number of people in the town, you'd think they could come to some consensus, but no. As is always the case, the biggest and loudest prevailed. The stage had been set before we arrived, so the loudest were already basically in charge by then."

"What did you do?" asked Lila.

"Nothing at first," answered Sean. "We were new. We had to get the lay of the land. Also, the problems weren't immediately apparent. It didn't seem like it was really any different from other town governments. As the town grew, the more powerful town council members slowly weeded out the weaker—or maybe I should say more honest—members, and replaced them with puppets who would go along with anything they decided. They decided that the power wasn't increasing fast enough. The pressure on Baxter to produce more than he was able became unbearable. Aaron and I— having electrical backgrounds in the Marines—tried to help, but it wasn't enough. They found Baxter one morning in bed, dead of a heart attack."

Sean continued. "Baxter had taught a few people some of what he was doing with the plant, so they were able to continue his work. But it was slower without his expertise. Eventually, though, the lights were stronger, and electricity began to filter its way into the town. People could use refrigerators, we had running water, and you actually started to hear music from some old record players people had found in antique shops."

He took a sip of tea and set it down on the table.

"The seat of power, if you want to call it that, changed hands a couple more times in just a couple of months. It was becoming quite chaotic. Dangerous, really. So I think people were actually relieved when the don came."

"The don?"

"You know, like in The Godfather. I don't think he really was a don. But he was some kind of Chicago mobster. Came in with about twenty tough guys. It didn't take long for him to be running the town. A lot of the townspeople embraced him, but it was clear where it was all heading. That's when we left. We tried hard to get Aaron to come with us. I could tell he was torn. He didn't want to stay there—it was just as obvious to him that while the don might bring temporary order, the long-term prospects were anything but rosy—but he was deeply in love and Emily wouldn't leave. Tiff was a few months old—old enough to travel—so we left. We heard about the Yellowstone community and decided to give it a try."

"Could the 'don' be capable of everything we've heard about ... and seen?" asked Lila.

"Don't know," answered Sean. "We weren't there long enough to know how far he would go, but I suppose anything is possible. But why? What does he gain by importing people?"

"Strength," replied Lila. "If he was really some kind of mobster, wouldn't his success depend on how large his organization is? And what better way to build loyalty than to dangle the enticement of electricity in front of people."

"Even if everyone hated him," added Ben, "they would probably do their best to tolerate him if it meant living with electricity. It's amazing what people can rationalize."

"Okay, I can accept that, I suppose, but why destroy other

towns? Why discard older people? I mean, we had some old people living in Paradise, and it didn't look as if he was going to do away with them."

"They were established already," answered Ben. "Politically it wouldn't be in his best interest to mess with the status quo. As for why he would destroy other towns, that's easy. It's the age-old story of conquerors. He's building an empire, and the only way to ensure success is to eliminate the competition."

"You seem to have a good grasp of history," noted Brittany.

"We read a lot of books in our years in the forest. At one point I got into a history kick. Not sure why, exactly. Nostalgia, maybe? It's like in one brief moment we wiped out thousands of years of struggle by man. I guess I just wanted to learn more about those struggles."

There was a moment of silence, as they all seemed to drift into memories of the past. The only sounds were the children playing in the background.

"Well," said Sean, finally. "Why don't you stay here tonight—in fact, as long as you need to. Can I assume you will be joining our community?"

"We would love to," said Lila. "I guess we have to think about finding a place to live."

"Don't worry about that," said Sean. "I have lots of lumber I've brought in from my forays, and lots of people who have promised me labor if I ever need it—their part of the barter. I don't need anything done, so I'll take them up on it for you. All you have to do is decide where you want to live. I can show you some choice locations that haven't been claimed yet. Some of the most beautiful spots you've ever seen."

"That's so kind of you," said Lila. Ben hadn't seen her this happy and excited in a long time.

"For the family of my best friend, I could never do enough. Which leads to a question ..."

"Am I going to make the journey to Paradise at some point?" asked Ben.

Sean nodded his head.

"I'm anxious to see my brother," he answered, "but for years I thought he was dead. My first priority has to be to make a home and decide how we can give back to the community. After that? Yeah, at some point I need to find him."

"When you do," said Sean. "I'll come with you."

I may have sounded nonchalant about my timetable for going to see Aaron, but in fact, it was burning a hole in my heart. And I knew that Lila was very aware of my need to find my brother. But as deep as the feelings were, my first responsibility was to my family. It wasn't just building the house. It was everything involved with survival: making sure we had plenty of wood for the fall and winter; gathering a small herd of animals—cows and goats for milking, chickens for eggs, and animals to provide meat if hunting got lean. And a million other things to do to get established.

No, I didn't foresee being able to find my brother until the following summer at the earliest.

Or so I thought...

Chapter 25

The spot they picked was one of the most spectacular places Ben had ever seen. In a valley virtually untouched by the earthquake—in fact, Ben was amazed at how little of Yellowstone had been affected by the quake. Maybe it had something to do with the strength of the rock underneath the ground, but he was just speculating. He knew nothing about geology. It could have just been a fluke thing.

In the valley were acres and acres of long grass, with a wide stream winding its way through the middle. Tall cliffs surrounded the valley, giving it the illusion of total privacy. Yet, at the same time, it was only a mile from the road that ran down to the town. Once they got Katie started in the school, traveling time would be less than an hour by horseback.

As promised by Sean, help was abundant. Once they decided on the location, it was only a few days before the frame of the house was constructed. A couple of weeks after that, it was livable. A few of the workers put up a small corral and barn. Ben and Lila were blown away by the enthusiasm they encountered among the neighbors. Nobody complained about the work and everyone seemed genuinely happy to welcome the newcomers.

The house was small, with two tiny bedrooms, a kitchen/dining room, and a small living room. Sean brought them a woodstove for the living room and a wood cook stove. A pantry was dug under the kitchen, with a ladder and trapdoor. The coolness of the pantry would take the place of a refrigerator to some extent. During the winter, the outdoors would be their freezer. One of their neighbors, Hank—Ben thought it an appropriate name for a cowboy—helped them round up some wild cattle. Hank had grown up on a ranch in Wyoming and knew his stuff when it came to cattle.

"You can let them out into the valley to graze," he explained. "In the beginning they might wander a bit, but if you keep bringing them back to the corral at night, they will eventually roam less and less."

Hank also brought them some chickens and pigs, as well as two goats.

"I have a surplus," he explained. "Over the last couple of years my pigs and chickens have multiplied. Don't need so many."

"I don't know my role yet in the community," explained Ben, "but if there is anything I can do for you, just give me a holler."

About a month after the house was finished, Ben was working to create space for a garden when he heard the approach of hoof beats. He looked around to see two bearded men sitting atop horses and looking down at him with frowns.

"You're getting pretty snobby in your old age," said one.

"You too good to look up old friends?"

And then the recognition set in. "Nick? Jason? Oh my God!"

The frowns turned to smiles and both men jumped off their horses and embraced Ben. Lila looked out the door of the house and gave a squeal. She ran out and hugged them.

Brittany was visiting that day—she and Lila had become best friends and spent a lot of time together—and she said, "You guys all know each other, I assume. Hey, Nick. Hi Jason."

"Hi Brit," responded Nick. "We do. We met a long time ago."

"They were the ones who warned us about the coming earthquake on the east coast, and suggested we settle in the Great Smoky Mountains," said Ben. He turned to his friends. "I can't believe you're here. We heard all about the plague back east and knew you had avoided it. Heard it from a guy we met named Frederick."

"Older guy with a limp and really bad body odor?"

"That's the one."

"We've been here about two years now. We're about four miles deeper in the wilderness. You know us, we like to keep to ourselves."

"We'd probably be there too," replied Ben, "but we need to be closer to the town so Katie can attend school. She needs that socialization."

Nick and Jason had changed dramatically in appearance. When Ben and Lila first met them, they still had that "civilized" look about them. Now they were both broader in the shoulders, muscular, and seemed totally at home in their new surroundings.

"We saw a veterinarian's office in town," Ben said to Jason. "Is that you?"

"I take my turn in there a couple of times a week. There's another vet, and he lives in town, so he's there most of the time."

The two men stayed a couple of hours and caught up. Of course, the question of Lila's eye patch was broached, so the story was related.

"That really sucks," said Jason. "But I've got to say that it makes you look even sexier."

"A high compliment, coming from a gay man," added Nick.

They all laughed.

"In all seriousness, it's really not so bad now," responded Lila. "I've gotten used to it. My ankle is almost more of a pain than my eye, but now that we do more riding than walking, the ankle doesn't act up so much. With everything that has happened to this world, if this is the worst I have to deal with, then I consider myself lucky."

They made arrangements to tour Nick and Jason's property as soon as possible, and the two men rode away. Nick was in search of a top-of-the-line telescope to do some stargazing. Since Sean hadn't run across one in his travels, they were going to scour the remains of the outlying towns themselves.

Ben, meanwhile, went back to work chopping wood for the winter and growing whatever vegetables he could this late in the season, unaware of the panic that was about to befall them.

*****

It came a few weeks later, as they were approaching the latter stages of summer. With the help of Sean and Brittany, Nick and Jason, and others, they were almost settled. The whole process took far less time than Ben could have hoped for. As in Monett, he was amazed at the contentment among the residents. Living alone for six years, Ben and Lila never experienced the transition between worlds with others, so it came as a surprise as to how settled the remaining population had become. Their only memories were of the shock and sadness they encountered everywhere they went that first year.

As much as they had liked their life in the Great Smoky Mountains, it couldn't compare to their new home. If that was Eden, this was certainly Heaven. Their view of the surrounding mountains was spectacular. The stream that ran through their property was wide enough to be considered a small river, and the meadow was lush with tall grass and colorful flowers. They had truly found their home. The transition was complete. The world they had once known was gone. They had long ago ceased to miss the "conveniences" of their old life, but now they had taken that next step, that of fully embracing the peace and tranquility that their new world offered. It was a significant change of consciousness—the meaning of which didn't escape them.

Katie was fully ensconced in school. The sole teacher in town turned out to be an enthusiastic middle-aged woman who somehow managed to creatively and effectively teach thirty children of diverse ages without anyone feeling lost. She challenged them, and they embraced it. She taught them about the world before the event so that they could understand where their parents had come from, as well as the attitudes and culture that made them who they were. But she also spent much time on the making of America—the early discoverers, the native peoples, and the migration west from the cities—making sure none of the students missed the similarities to their own life. In the process, Katie formed numerous friendships, proving to Ben that Lila was correct in her dreams for their daughter.

At seven, Katie had become fairly independent, and would often ride by herself to friends' houses—those who weren't more than a couple of miles away. At first, these were the few times when Ben missed one of the remnants of his old life—cell phones. How nice it would have been to be able to have Katie call when she arrived at a friend's house. But even that anxiety dissipated when he saw the ease with which she was able to get around.

It was a beautiful sunny day when she disappeared. She was going on a picnic with her best friend Sophie, and Sophie's mom, Brenda. It was nothing unusual. Katie and Sophie spent a lot of time together, usually in the presence of Brenda or Lila. Although Lila didn't feel the closeness with Brenda that she did with Brittany, they were good friends nonetheless, and she was forever grateful for the interest Brenda showed in Katie. In Brenda's hands, Katie would always be safe.

Which is why she wasn't overly concerned when dusk began to fall and Katie still hadn't returned. But as darkness settled in, Lila found an uneasiness taking over. This was totally unlike Katie. Unless arrangements had been made ahead of time, she wouldn't have spent the night at Sophie's. She voiced her concern to Ben.

"I'll take a ride over," he said. "I'm sure she's fine. They probably let the time get away from them. It's getting darker earlier now. Maybe it caught them by surprise."

"I know. I just have a feeling though. I can't verbalize it, but it just doesn't feel right. Please be careful."

It had been a long time since Lila had uttered those words. It brought back scary memories for Ben. He saddled up Moose, hooked a strong flashlight to the pommel, and set off to Brenda's house. It was only a mile and a half away, and the trail was wide and smooth, but it was a bit spooky making the ride at night. In general, they avoided night riding. Besides the danger of unseen branches or holes and the occasional nocturnal hunter, it was especially hard for Lila, putting a strain on her one good eye.

He arrived at Brenda's house a short time later. Frank, Brenda's husband, was pacing the porch. He looked up when he saw Ben, the disappointment obvious.

"Was hoping you were Brenda," he said.

"Do you know where they went?" asked Ben.

"Said they were going to have a picnic over on West Slope. Was going to give them another ten minutes, then I was going to go look for them."

"Let's go together," said Ben. "Go saddle up."

West Slope was not on the official Yellowstone map. It had been named by the residents of Rock Creek. A gentle slope at the base of a rocky point, West Slope was a favorite picnicking spot, with beautiful views and lots of shade. It was a good place to observe herds of bison and elk. Less than four miles from Brenda's house at the end of a well-worn trail, it would be difficult to get lost coming from or going to West Slope.

Once Frank was saddled, the two men took off down the

trail, going more cautiously than they would in the light. They were hoping to run into the group somewhere along the way, but they arrived at their destination having seen no one.

Ben shone the flashlight around, seeing no traces of the picnickers.

"Over here," called Frank.

Ben rode over to where Frank was standing next to his horse. Now the worry was real. Next to a large rock was a bag containing sandwiches and drinks—all untouched.

"What the hell is going on?" asked Frank, a hollow tone to his voice.

Ben didn't answer. He was shining his light over the whole area, hoping to find a clue. When he saw it, his blood ran cold.

Mixed among the footprints and hoof prints in the dirt below the rock were very distinct tire tracks. As Ben raised his light, he saw the tracks trail away in the tall grass away from the picnic site.

A truck. Ben knew. A truck had taken his daughter. And there was no doubt where it was going. And now there was no doubt where Ben was going.

He was heading for Nebraska, and Nebraska was going to feel his wrath.

Chapter 26

"It's time to go."

The truth was, it was long past the time they should have gone. Aaron knew it, but he also knew that they couldn't leave until Emily was ready. He held her as the tears rolled down her dark cheeks.

"I know," she said, her voice choking. "It's just going to be so hard to leave them."

"Some will be coming with us."

"But not all. What will happen to the kids left behind?"

"It's not like they don't have parents or families. They will adjust. It's what we've all been doing for almost eight years—adjusting."

She nodded. Even with the sorrow clearly etched in her face, Aaron found her beautiful. Born in Haiti, Emily came to the U.S. when she was three, her parents seeking a better life. Although they never found the pot of gold they were hoping for, they provided for and loved their daughter, allowing her to grow up in a stable home—even while living in the slums of

New York. The proudest day in their life came the day their daughter graduated from Columbia with her degree in teaching. She stayed in New York working in the inner city—a young, idealistic, popular teacher.

She had an ever-so-slight accent, inherited from listening to her parents speak, as she had no memories herself of Haiti. Despite Emily being five years older than Aaron and much more cerebral, the spark was there from the moment they met. They were deeply in love. With the world the way it was, neither felt the need to get formally married—was there even such a thing anymore? Being together was enough for them. They knew it was for real and forever.

"Maybe by the time we go we can convince some of the others to come with us," she suggested hopefully.

"I think we've put out enough feelers. Those who are going to come have already committed. So far we've been able to keep it quiet. I don't hold out a lot of hope that it'll stay that way much longer. That's why we have to go soon—within the week."

"What do you think will happen if the don finds out?" asked Emily.

It was a subject they had purposely avoided up until now. But it was a valid—and disturbing—question. What would the don do? He was clearly evil, a quality no one saw at first. Once people began to recognize the dark side of him, they just assumed he was unstable. Instability had certainly become part of the picture, but he also knew exactly what he was doing, and he was calculating enough to take his time in letting it come out.

He had fooled them all. He came into Paradise putting

across a toughness and an organization sorely needed. He wasn't popular—hardly a concern to him—and he wasn't trusted by some, but the town was in disarray and everyone knew it. Someone needed to bring order or all of Baxter's work—his dream to restore power—would be for naught.

So while he wasn't liked, the townspeople saw him as a necessary evil. They just didn't realize the depth of that evil. Even Aaron, his senses honed by his Marine training, failed to pick up that side of the don at first.

The truck convoys were sent out at first simply to gather supplies, so when the first few trucks arrived with newcomers to the town, they naturally thought the people in the trucks had come willingly. Truth was, in the beginning they did. They were told about the electricity and it was enough to convince most. After all, they had been without the conveniences of their former life far too long. They equated electricity with normalcy. Aaron even went on a few of those early supply runs. The survivors they ran into seemed so grateful to be invited to come back with them.

But things changed. Besides the goons the don had brought with him, he enlisted others of questionable repute. Some were from the gangs that roamed the countryside. An offer of regular food and shelter was enough for many of them to join his force. These men took over most of the truck runs. After that, Aaron began to notice that as the number of survivors who returned in the trucks began to increase, many of them seemed to object to having been brought there. And more recently, when he began to hear that force was being used, he knew it was time to leave. He couldn't fight them, and he was concerned about Emily's safety. He had wanted to go soon after the don came, and really wanted to leave with Sean. But Emily felt she would be abandoning her students. The town's population had swelled to over five hundred, and somehow she was still the only teacher. She had forty students of varying ages to teach. What would happen to them if she left?

As sad as she was, Aaron knew she was finally ready. It would soon become dangerous, and they had no idea what the don had in store for the future.

Electricity had been restored. Lights worked. Refrigerators and electric stoves worked—though not all of them. The older the better—even some old VCRs with equally old TVs were working and people were watching movies and regaling in the nostalgia. DVD players and the newer TVs were still silent. It had something to do with the sophistication of the later circuit boards. Aaron had been responsible for getting some of the electronics working, but he wasn't sure many of them would ever work again. Even some of the ones old enough to work had rusted out over time.

There was also the question of the supplies that were brought in. They were freely distributed to the townspeople from a small warehouse—the "company store" some people began to call it—but even that was subtly changing. More and more, the residents were relying on that warehouse. They all had gardens, but were doing less hunting and gathering on their own. Aaron suspected that the don was counting on this growing reliance. Somewhere down the line, it was going to come back and bite the townspeople in the ass.

So yes, the town had electricity, but he was beginning to wonder if it was worth all the work. So much attention was being put on getting the town "on line," something else was missing. It felt to him that everyone was trying too hard to relive the past.

Suddenly, a week wasn't soon enough.

"We have to leave tomorrow or the next day," he announced.

Emily cocked her head in a questioning way.

"A week might be too late. I can't explain it. I just know it."

"I believe you. I'll teach class tomorrow while you let those who are coming know. We'll leave tomorrow night. Can you steal the trucks?"

Aaron appreciated that when a decision was made, Emily was on board. Her tears were in the past. Now was the time for action.

But it was just a day too late. The next morning as Aaron and Emily were leaving the house, four of the don's men met them at the door. As usual, they were well armed.

"Aaron, the don wants to see you."

"It'll have to be later. Tell him I'll stop by."

"Now." The weapons came out.

They were serious.

"Can you give me a minute?"

"Nope. When he says now, he means now. Let's go."

He touched Emily's hand, knowing that they had waited too long. The don had heard of their plans. Her face showed fear, and Aaron knew it wasn't unfounded. Their chances of leaving now gone, that was no longer Aaron's greatest concern. Knowing the don's irrationality, he knew that Emily was afraid she'd never see him again.

Yeah, well that wasn't going to happen. Aaron had led a quiet life in Paradise and had purposely stayed in the background. But it was time to step out of the background. He hadn't become a Marine for the fun of it. He had prepared for life on the front lines in Afghanistan and was an expert marksman. More importantly for the situation he was probably about to face, he had become highly skilled in the martial arts. And in the Marines, you don't learn the martial arts to win tournaments. You learn them for one simple purpose—to kill.

Chapter 27

Marco "the don" Bolli was a fraud. Not only was he not a don, he wasn't even Marco Bolli. His real name was Henry Young. And now he was in trouble. He had gone too far, and he knew it. But there was no way to undo the damage. To reverse things now would make him appear weak and indecisive.

He never should have forced people to join his town. The real Marco Bolli would never have been so heavy-handed. Bolli had a grace about him. He could be vicious, but he could also be charming. People wanted to be around him. But Bolli was dead, killed in the event like so many others.

Henry Young was a two-bit thug who had worked for Bolli. More intelligent than most thugs, he had actually gone to college and had real goals. He saw the success that Bolli had enjoyed as a big-time Chicago mobster and wanted some of it for himself. In reality, Bolli wasn't really a don. In fact, Henry didn't even know if there had even been any old-style dons anymore. But if not, Bolli would have been the closest thing to it.

So when the "big bang"—as Henry called it—happened, and he found himself the only one of Bolli's men alive, he did the logical thing. He became Marco Bolli. Bolli was well-known in Chicago, but not well-photographed, so it was simple to assume the role of Bolli. Who would know?

In the few months after the big bang, he ran across a number of surviving low-lifes who were desperate enough to latch onto someone with leadership qualities—especially Marco Bolli himself! Over the next few years, Henry made the transition from lowly thug to a man of power and respect. Since he really didn't have the class and intelligence to do exactly what Bolli would have done in various situations, he winged it. And it worked. After all, he had long since convinced everybody that he was Bolli, so why wouldn't they accept any decision he made?

Eventually he heard about Paradise and he knew it was for him. He was bored in the suburbs—he had vacated Chicago early on for a magnificent mansion in Lake Forest. There was nothing to do any more and no way to flaunt his power. And he liked to flaunt his power. His followers were getting restless and in time he would lose his control over them. He needed a new challenge. More importantly, he craved the electricity that a move to Paradise promised. Frankly, this new world sucked big-time. He wanted some conveniences, starting with electricity. He had accumulated a small fleet of older trucks, thanks to a nearby military base, and he had the foresight to recognize the importance of stockpiling gasoline. So his fleet included tanker trucks filled to the brim with gas.

When he made the decision to head to Paradise, his troops were ready. He told them the stories he had heard about the electricity, and promised them that he would take over the town, making sure his loyal followers reaped the benefits.

When he arrived in Paradise, he played it well, coming on as strong and decisive, while managing to piss off as few people as possible. It was quite easy, really, to take over the town. It was already in a chaotic state. Everyone wanted control, but all had a different opinion as to the direction the town should take. Henry—as Bolli—swooped in with his little army and made some quick decisions. Everyone seemed happy with a strong leader.

The problem came when Henry started to suffer from the paranoia often associated with power. It was easy for him to take over the town, but the town was still small—just a few hundred residents. What if someone even stronger, with an even larger force than Henry had, heard about the electricity and wanted in on the deal? The logic of that fear was baseless— ridiculous, really—but when you lived your whole life in a profession filled with paranoia, life, logic went out the window. And Henry realized too late that that was the difference between him and the real Marco. Marco would have taken in the whole situation and would have developed the town slowly, relying on his charisma and intelligence to develop loyalty. He would have known that the chances of an even larger force than his own showing up would be pretty implausible, judging by the state of the landscape after the earthquakes. No, the real Marco Bolli wouldn't have botched it up. The fake one had.

What began as supply-gathering forays and scouting missions to recruit new town members eventually turned into instances of kidnapping. Power was in numbers, so the larger the population of Paradise, the less likely Henry would have a fight on his hands with some outside force. It had even worked at first. Many of the people brought to Paradise against their wishes actually ended up happy they had come, their memories of life with electricity rekindled. It gave him the confidence that he was right in his decision.

But then his goons became more aggressive and some lives were lost. Things were getting out of control. When a couple of his patrols failed to return—including the large one he sent to Monett—fear set in and he began to make stupid decisions. He was losing his grip, not just on his authority, but to some extent on his own sanity. It was inevitable, though. He was never prepared to be a leader of so many, and the pressure had finally taken its toll. But the greater the paranoia became, the less he was content in ruling a town. No, he needed more territory under his control, and it didn't matter how he obtained it.

And now he was hearing rumors that some were planning to leave Paradise. He wasn't going to let that happen. If he let them go, the decision might someday come back to haunt him. They could use their knowledge of the town to get back at it— at him—with others. Supposedly the ringleader was Aaron, the one person in town he steered clear of. The one person he had feared from the very beginning. Aaron had never been a problem, but he had a quiet strength that bothered Henry, the strength of a real leader. If he allowed Aaron to defect with a group, it could destroy Henry's control over the town. And he could never allow that to happen. He had sent his men to get Aaron and put an end to the defection. Now the only question was: What to do with him?

Chapter 28

Katie wasn't scared. In fact, she couldn't really remember ever being scared. She looked over at Sophie and her mom and couldn't understand why they were crying. Not that she had never cried before. She cried once when she fell down a steep slope of rocks. She cried when Ralph got hurt on their trip and when her dad fell in the big hole. And she cried when the fire drove them from their home. But it wasn't for the house burning down, it was for all the animals who died in the fire. Her mom said a lot of the animals escaped, but she knew it wasn't true. It made her so sad.

But not this. Katie knew they weren't really in danger. It wasn't just because the men had assured them of it, but she had heard her mom and dad talking about the men and the trucks many times with Sean. She also remembered the men in the other trucks by the ravine. Her dad had talked to her about that afterwards. She also heard all the noise when the trucks came to their town.

No, she wasn't scared. She wasn't even really angry. She

grew up in the woods. Things happened. Her dad always taught her that she shouldn't panic. She should just look for a way to solve the problem. She knew from experience that part of the problem would be solved for her. They were taking her away from her mom and dad and from her new home. Her mom and dad wouldn't be very happy about that. Not at all.

She was mad about one thing. They had Scooby and the other two horses tied to the back of the truck. They weren't going very fast—an easy speed for the horses—but it wasn't fair to them. They didn't get to rest and they had to smell the stinky smoke that was coming out the back of the truck. She wasn't happy about that at all. She was happy though, that she had left Ralph at home. The men might have hurt him.

The picnic had been fun. Katie and Sophie were best friends, and Sophie's mom was nice. They were having fun— until the men in the trucks came. The men told them they were taking them to a wonderful place that had electricity. Katie had heard of electricity before—her mom and dad had explained it, but she didn't really understand it. Anyway, she didn't want to go to another town, especially without her mom and dad. She told them that, but they didn't care. They just kept saying how much she'd like it there. How would they know?

She had liked Monett, but it was better here. She had more friends here—especially Sophie. She also got to see Scooby everyday—he lived in a barn next to the house and she rode him all the time. Monett had that ugly town next to it, the one nobody lived in. They called it the "old town." Katie hadn't been allowed to ride Scooby into the old town. But that was okay. She didn't want to go there anyway. She always rode the other way. But it was so flat there. She could ride fast, but she never felt like she really went anywhere. It was so much prettier here. So much to see and to explore.

There were also no ugly towns in Yellowstone. It was just hills and grass and forest and lots of places to ride. There were a lot of animals too, which she liked. She stayed away from the bears and bison—the bison could be mean—and she heard that there were mountain lions, but she hadn't seen any. She couldn't wait to see one though.

Her mom and dad let her ride alone. They trusted her. After all, she would be eight next summer. She always kept her crossbow with her—she could even load it herself now!—and hung it on Scooby or over her back like a backpack when she rode. She hadn't had to use it yet on her own—only when she went hunting with her dad. She was good! Almost as good as him with his big crossbow. Now, her crossbow was in a bag on Scooby. The men hadn't seen it. That was good, because these men were bad. That much was clear. Suddenly Katie felt that it was her responsibility to protect Sophie and her mom, because they were so scared. She held Sophie's hand. Sophie's mom had a rifle with her at the picnic, but the men took it, and Sophie didn't have any weapons—Katie wasn't sure why. It was up to Katie. But how would she get the crossbow off Scooby without the men seeing? And then what would she do? She saw her mom shoot that man by the ravine. Could she shoot someone? She shot animals for food all the time, and she had shot the dog that attacked Ralph. She imagined her dad's voice: Don't panic. Stay calm.

After a few hours they stopped the trucks for a rest. That was good. Katie really had to pee. Afterward, she wiped down Scooby with a rag she found in the truck, quietly singing the song her dad had taught her: "Scooby Dooby Doo, where are you, we've got some work to do now." There was grass, and the horses were eating. The men were sitting in the grass smoking. She reached around Scooby and took the bag with her crossbow off. She was going to try to sneak it into the truck, but one of the men saw her.

"Whatcha got there?" he asked, standing up.

"My toys," replied Katie. "They were bouncing on Scooby. I think it hurts him. I was putting them in the truck."

"Scooby?"

"My horse. I named him after a big dog named Scoo…"

"Scooby Doo. Yeah, I know. I used to watch it. In Paradise we have a Scooby Doo tape. You can watch it on the VCR."

None of that made any sense to Katie.

"Yeah, go ahead and put it in the truck."

Katie quickly lifted it into the truck, then looked at the man. He looked familiar. He caught her looking at him.

"Whatcha looking at?"

"I've seen you before." And then it came to her. "A long time ago. You were with some other men. You came to our camp and my mom and dad gave you some food. You were hungry."

He stared blankly at her.

"I don't think my dad trusted you. He made you put your guns in a pile and gave them back to you the next morning. My mom knew one of the other men, I think."

He remembered. He remembered all too clearly. He also remembered the names of her parents and the stories about them.

"Ben and Lila? They're your parents?"

She nodded her head.

"Shit!" He turned to the one in charge. "Cap'n. We've gotta go."

"I was about to. But what's the hurry?"

"Remember the stories about that couple back in the early days? Ben and Lila?" The captain nodded. "Remember I said I'd met them about a year-and-a-half ago or so?"

"And?"

"We just took their daughter. They are going to be fucking pissed."

"Wait, these girls don't belong to that woman?"

"Not this one."

"Shit. Well, I'm not too worried. We've got a big head start. We can go over the ravines, they have to find a way around. We'll be back in Paradise long before they can catch up. And I don't care what the stories are about them. They can't take on a whole town."

They were herded back into the truck and were on their way within minutes. Katie could tell that the second man, the one called Cap'n, was scared too. Good, she thought.

The going was slow. Sometimes they could drive almost an hour without stopping to skirt torn up ground, or to put their bridge over a ravine. Other times it seemed they wandered for hours trying to find level ground again. They passed small towns and a couple of cities, all dark and foreboding. Katie shivered as they passed a particularly ugly town.

"Why did people live there?" she asked in amazement.

"They didn't always look like that," answered Brenda. Katie noticed that Sophie's mom didn't seem scared anymore. "They used to be busy and light. People would shop and go to restaurants and go to the movies..." she stopped. Katie and Sophie were staring at her blankly.

"Well, you'll just have to trust me. They were lively places."

"Where did they keep their horses?" asked Katie.

Brenda chuckled. "Most people didn't have horses."

The conversation deteriorated from there.

They arrived in Paradise about a week after they were picked up. The rear of the truck had become very uncomfortable and they were anxious to move around. They drove into the town in the early evening, and Katie finally saw the "electricity" that she had heard so much about. Houses had lights in the windows and on the porches, and there were big lights that overhung the street. The lights were interesting, but what fascinated her even more was the sound. It was music, but it wasn't coming from live instruments. At first she liked it, but as they approached the center of town it became louder and from many places—and it was all different. It was so loud and so different, it almost blended into one noisy mess. She put her hands over her ears.

"I don't like this," she said to Brenda. Katie noticed that Sophie had her hands over her ears as well, and had her eyes scrunched shut.

"It is loud," agreed Brenda, although she realized that to Katie and Sophie it must have sounded like a cacophony of noise. To Brenda, who grew up in an age of loud and diversified music, it wasn't nearly as annoying.

The truck stopped in front of a wooden building with a sign out front that read Paradise School.

"Here's where you can spend the night," said the Captain,

opening the tail gate. They climbed out, Katie clutching her bag of "toys." "We have a few beds set aside for newcomers. The school's teacher will get you settled, then tomorrow we'll find a permanent place for you. Welcome to Paradise. You'll like it here. It's almost like the old days. Here she is now."

A pretty black woman approached them. She tried to smile at them, but Katie didn't think she looked very happy.

"All yours," said the Captain, who then headed off to a large official-looking building.

"Hi, I'm Emily. Let me get you settled."

When they were inside the building and the door was shut, Emily flicked a switch and an overhead light went on. Katie and Sophie both gasped.

A hint of a smile came over Emily's face. "First time?" she asked, looking at Brenda.

"First time."

Emily turned serious and her voice lowered. "You've come at a bad time," she said to Brenda. While Sophie looked around, Katie listened intently to every word.

"We didn't want to come at all," replied Brenda. "We were kidnapped. We live in Yellowstone."

"My partner and I were going to leave today, but they took him away yesterday and I haven't heard anything. That's the whole reason we were leaving. They are now forcing people to come here—I'm not sure why. My partner says he heard it's to increase the population to prevent others from attacking us, but that's just paranoid thinking, as far as I'm concerned." She stopped, then looked at Brenda. "Did you say Yellowstone? Do you know a couple by the names of Sean and Brittany?"

"You mean Uncle Sean and Aunt Brittany?" asked Katie.

"I guess so. Sean is your uncle?"

"They just call them that," answered Brenda. "They do have some connection though, but I'm not sure what it is." She looked at Katie.

"Uncle Sean's friend is my daddy's brother. But I haven't met him yet. His name is Aaron."

"Oh my God! Is your daddy's name Ben?"

Katie nodded her head.

"And Ben and my husband Frank will be on their way here to get us," said Brenda. "I'm sure they'll bring others, including Sean."

Emily moved closer to Brenda and her voice dropped to a whisper, but Katie could hear her anyway.

"The people controlling this town have a lot of men and a lot of guns. And even those who aren't part of that group, if they think they are being attacked, they'll fight too. If Sean and Ben and your husband come into this town on a rescue mission, it's going to be a bloodbath."

Katie saw Brenda's eyes tear up.

"A lot of people are going to die," said Emily.

Chapter 29

Less than a hundred miles west of Paradise, Ben and Lila and the rest of their group were allowing themselves an hour respite. They had made good time, thanks to a few lucky breaks—including some ravines that didn't extend as far as they had thought, allowing them to circumvent them more quickly—and the combined knowledge of the searchers. Many, like Nick, Jason, and Sean, had been that way before, and remembered some of the less damaged areas.

In all, there were seventeen riders. It was the best they could do in a short amount of time. Ben, Lila, and Frank were anxious to get going, but all had the foresight to know that there was strength in numbers. The sheer size of Yellowstone prevented word from spreading too quickly, but even so, in twelve hours they had their group of seventeen. They could have had more, given another day, but they had waited long enough. They knew that Katie, Brenda, and Sophie wouldn't be harmed, but that brought them little comfort. Time was of the essence.

They were well-armed. Over the years, most survivors had managed to accumulate an over-abundance of weapons. Ironically, given their history, Ben and Lila, with their one rifle and one pistol each, along with Ben's crossbow, were among the least armed of the group.

"Will they be ready for us?" asked Ben, as they sat by a stream soaking their feet while the horses drank from the crystal clear water. Ralph sat beside him, obviously missing Katie's presence.

"They'll be ready," answered Sean. Another man, Simpson—Ben wasn't sure if it was a first or last name—nodded in agreement. Like Sean, he had spent time in Paradise, leaving about a year after the former Marine.

"They'll keep the townspeople in the dark—no pun intended—but the don's goons will be ready. No doubt about that," said Simpson.

"Any particular reason, or are they just always ready?" asked Ben.

"A little of both," answered Simpson. "They always have people watching the roads just as a matter of course, but in this case he'll have extra men on. They've never come this close to Yellowstone before, and the don is totally paranoid about Yellowstone. He's forever expecting an attack from us—which is, of course, absurd—but this will just fuel the fire in his mind."

"Here's what I don't get," said Lila. "Okay, so we're not the same society we once were, but we can't be that far removed from who we used to be. I know that in some of the third-world countries it wasn't unusual for one town to attack another. But this was ... is ... the United States. That kind of thing just didn't happen. Why are they afraid of it now?"

"Because we are a third world country now," answered Nick. "We've all encountered the violence that sprang up after the event—you and Ben probably even more than any of us. We always hope that in times of disaster people will come together and help each other. While there is certainly much evidence of that, I've been dismayed that there wasn't more. We touched on this when we first met."

"I remember," said Lila.

"I think the country—or the world—is left with three distinct groups, a distinction that is more clear now than it was in that year after the event. First are those like us, who are determined to maintain a civilized society. Second are those who care only about their own survival—which includes people like the don and the misfits of society he has assembled under him. The third group is the least predictable. It's the people who go whichever way the wind is blowing. They are still lost, even now. In essence, they died a long time ago, but just don't know it."

"Some of those in your third group ended up in Paradise," said Sean. "Their thirst for electricity and for a sense of normalcy drew them there. Some had even learned to live in the new world reasonably well before they found Paradise. Frankly, I think many of them regressed once they found some of those comforts again."

Nick nodded in agreement. "And if they feel that lifestyle threatened in any way, they'll fight to keep it. Many of them probably tried to do the right thing at first, but finally just got sick of it all. Their moral compass went out of whack and they no longer cared about much of anything. Their own survival trumped everything else."

Ben started to dry his feet in anticipation of the ride ahead. "So what you're saying is that we really can't trust anyone there."

"There are some really good people in Paradise," said Sean. "People like us who are trying. They'll be smart enough to make themselves scarce in the event of violence. We won't see them until it's all over. So to answer your question: yes, I wouldn't trust anyone."

There was nothing to be said to that, so they all quietly saddled their horses.

They rode for three days, the stress increasing with every mile. Sean kept assuring Ben and Lila that Katie would be okay, but it did little to calm them. Ben wasn't fearful, he was angry.

I don't exactly know what I was expecting when we left our cabin by the lake. I was hoping that things had changed for the better, with people thinking about the future of the country. In so many ways I was disappointed. Was I hoping for too much? The Monett settlement existed, as did Yellowstone, and that brought me hope. I was sure that there had to be others, as well. And then there was Paradise. The most advanced town technologically was also the most corrupt. Just a coincidence? I was beginning to realize that this wasn't nearly enough time to purge the world of the scum. It was really going to be up to Katie's generation to turn the world around. In the meantime, I would do my part ... starting with the don.

*****

They were on a bluff across the river from Paradise. The

horses were tethered below, and all seventeen were watching the town through binoculars.

"What's the city adjacent to Paradise?" asked Ben.

"Scottsbluff," answered Sean. "It's nothing more than a burned out shell now. I took a few trips into the city. It seemed to catch the brunt of the devastation more than some other cities I encountered. Nothing left there. The power plant and the surrounding section of town was somehow spared the worst of it." He pointed down at Paradise. "So most of the town of Paradise is really just a trailer park, probably built for the workers at the plant. Mixed in are a few permanent buildings. It's actually not bad looking and they fixed it up pretty well."

"Where would they hold Katie, Sophie, and Brenda?"

"They wouldn't be 'holding' them." Sean made quotation marks with his fingers. "Believe it or not, it's not a prison. Despite their methods, people aren't prisoners. They are free to go. Problem is, once they get there, there's no place for them to go. That's why most of them settle in to life there. Then they get used to having electricity and don't want to go. So to answer your question, I don't know where they would be. Could be anywhere. Probably they are staying with someone for now."

"What's the newer building in the center," asked Lila.

"The town hall. Home of the don. Used to be the offices for the power plant."

"So that's our destination."

"Is our goal to get Brenda, Katie, and Sophie, or to seek revenge on the don?" asked Sean. "I just want to make sure our purpose is clear."

"Our goal," stated Ben, "is to get our families back and

convince Aaron to leave. Once that has been accomplished, my goal is to take care of the don. He's caused too much suffering already, and we will always be wondering if he'll make a return trip to Yellowstone. He's got to go. Then maybe the residents of Paradise can get their act together and make it a thriving town—without the paranoia."

"Just checking," replied Sean. "I'm with you on both counts. Now, we should figure out a plan."

*****

Two hours later, Nick and Jason entered the town of Paradise on horseback by way of the main road. Construction had started on what looked suspiciously like a checkpoint or guardhouse, and they were greeted by a man in uniform carrying a rifle.

"Welcome to Paradise," he said seriously. "Everyone is welcome. You passing through or thinking of staying?"

"Wow," said Nick, looking around. "The stories are true. You really do have power. That's awesome. But to answer your question, it depends. Just came from Ohio. We think a friend of ours might be living here. If so, chances are we'll stay ... if you'll have us."

"Like I said, everyone's welcome. Who's your friend?"

"Her name's Emily. Tall black woman. Good looking. Know her?"

It was decided that Nick and Jason wouldn't bring up Aaron's name. As the popular school teacher, Emily was the safer bet.

"I do. Do you know the guy she's with?" Nick knew he

was fishing. Was Aaron causing trouble? He had never met Aaron, but being Ben's brother, he wouldn't be surprised.

"She's with a guy? Good for her. Knew she'd hook up with someone eventually."

Satisfied with the answer, the guard pointed to a two-story prefab building on the next street. "That's the school. She's teaching today."

"Hey, thanks. This is really exciting."

"No problem. Wait a sec. You came all the way from Ohio and all you have is a small backpack and your rifle?"

"God, no. We've got more stuff than you could ever imagine. I'm surprised our horses haven't collapsed under the weight. We made camp about five miles up the road. Decided to leave it there, rather than carry it all in here with us. If we decide to stay, we'll go get it."

Once again the guard was appeased.

As they rode away and were out of earshot from the guard, Jason said, "You really are quite the liar. Do you lie to me that much?"

"No," Nick answered with a grin. "But then, I might be lying."

"Hear that God-awful music?" asked Jason. It was coming from every direction. "I hear rap, I hear folk, rock, you name it. They making up for lost time? It's like they want to blare it to prove they have the ability to play it. Wow! It would drive me insane."

They reached the school. It must have been recess, as they heard yelling and laughing behind the building. They walked around to the back. A playground was adjacent to a large field. The younger children were playing on swing sets and bars, while the older children played kickball in the field. Overseeing them was an attractive black woman. She noticed them and walked over.

"Can I help you?"

"Nick! Jason!" Katie and Sophie ran over from the swing set and hugged the two men. Nick and Jason quickly looked around to see if anyone was watching.

Nick whispered to the girls, "Shh, don't tell anyone we're here."

Both girls picked up on it immediately, looked around as Nick and Jason had done, and ran back to the swings.

Emily got it as well. "You're from Yellowstone." It was a statement.

"We are. Hi Emily. I'm Nick and this is Jason. We're with Sean, Aaron's brother Ben, Brenda's husband, and ten or twelve others. We came to get Brenda, Katie, and Sophie. Hopefully you and Aaron will come too."

A tear rolled down Emily's cheek. She proceeded to tell them of preparing to leave and Aaron being taken away. "They are keeping him in the town hall. They let me visit him yesterday. He's okay. I think they are just trying to figure out what to do with him. I'm afraid they are going to kill him. What other choice do they have? They could banish him, or both of us, but it might backfire on them. I think they are planning to quietly kill him and dispose of his body. They probably figure people will just forget about him."

"Which puts your life in danger too," said Jason.

"Yes."

"Well, we're going to get you out," said Nick.

"They are ready for you. They know Katie is Ben and Lila's

daughter. That scares them. They have men everywhere."

"Do you know how many?"

"Somewhere around forty."

"We're coming in tonight. Hopefully we can sneak you, Brenda, Katie, and Sophie out. I'm sure Sean and Ben will have a plan to break out Aaron. Where will you all be tonight?"

"At my trailer." She gave the directions.

"Okay. Be ready."

"It's going to be a violent night tonight, isn't it?"

"I see no way around it."

"We'll be ready."

Chapter 30

Nick and Jason spent another hour looking around, observing the people and the activities in Paradise. They were oddly disturbed by what they saw, but couldn't put their finger on exactly what it was. They left the same way they came in. The guard from earlier was still on duty.

"Find Emily?"

"We did. We're going to stay. I have to say that we didn't need much convincing. I think we'd already made up our minds. We're going to head back and get our stuff and we'll be back in the morning. I notice a lot of guys in uniform—like you. Is this part army base?"

"Nah. But we have the only electricity in the country, far as we know. We have to protect it."

"I hear ya. See you tomorrow."

They rode off, anxious to get back, but trying to look as nonchalant as possible.

"I hear ya?" said Jason, once they were a safe distance away.

"That was my hick voice, just showing that I'm one of the boys."

"Yeah, well. It doesn't fit you. Knock it off."

*****

"Impressions?" asked Ben when Nick and Jason returned.

"Sadness," said Nick. "People looked unhappy."

"Not unhappy," Jason clarified. "Suspicious. Kind of like a kid with a toy who doesn't want to share. They weren't very welcoming. Nothing overt. It was just the feeling I got. Kind of unsettling."

"That's not how it was in the beginning," said Sean, "but I don't doubt that it's how it is now."

"Because of the don?" asked Lila.

"Yes and no. It was heading that way before he showed up, but he probably exacerbated the situation."

"What does the firepower look like?" asked Ben.

"Lots of uniforms. Emily says around forty," said Nick.

"They won't be all on duty at night," said Sean. "Hard to travel at night. They know that, so they won't go overboard. I'd guess no more than fifteen or so. I say we go in quietly, get Brenda and the kids, and beat it out of there. Once they're safe we go for Aaron. Any objections?"

"You're the professional," said Ben. "Whatever you think."

"Small group. Me, Ben, and Frank ... "

"And me," put in Lila.

Sean looked at her and nodded. "We leave at midnight. Everyone else is backup. Leave two people here with the horses and Ralph—I think it would be safer if he didn't come—then everyone else quietly make your way down closer to the town. If all hell breaks loose, shoot anyone in a uniform. If things are going bad for us, get out of here. At that point it will be a losing battle for all of us. Got it?"

They reluctantly agreed, but running wasn't something they had any intention of doing.

It was already dusk. They took the time to rest. Below them the town had come alive with lights and music. From what Ben could see, there was no conservation of electricity, nor did there need to be. The power plant was humming away. It seemed that they had finally harnessed it to its fullest.

Finally, midnight arrived. Most of the music had died, and many of the house lights were off. It was time to go.

"You going to be able to see okay?" Sean asked Lila.

"I'll be fine," she answered curtly.

"Sorry."

"No, I'm sorry. I'm just anxious."

"I understand."

They started down the hill, having found a grassy slope that made the traveling easier. When they reached the edge of the river, they held their guns above their heads and crossed. During the day from their position on the hill, they had been able to determine the shallowest spot to cross. It was chest deep most of the way, but they made it without incident. They came up behind the power plant and took a moment to prepare for the second phase.

With Sean leading the way, they crept through the town, skirting street lights and staying behind buildings. When they reached Emily's trailer, Sean quietly knocked on her door. She opened it and the four of them entered. Emily had woken the kids up earlier, knowing what was coming. Katie ran to Ben and Lila, while Frank embraced his family. Not a word was uttered — Emily had prepared them well.

Sean gave Emily a hug. "You ready?"

"What about Aaron?"

"As soon as we get all of you out, we're going for him."

Everyone was packed up. Katie had her crossbow loaded, to which Ben and Lila said nothing. What could they say? She may have been seven, but she was mature far beyond her years. When Ben was young, if he held a dangerous weapon like that, his mother would have said, 'put it down. You'll knock someone's eye out with it.' Now, that was exactly the purpose.

"Let's go."

He opened the door silently and led the procession down the three steps to the road. They didn't get ten feet when a half a dozen flashlights suddenly turned on, illuminating them.

A voice called out, "We figured someone would. ..." A blast from Sean's M-16 cut him down in mid-sentence. Frank and Ben opened fire. Lila pushed Brenda and the girls down into a storm drain next to the house and took some shots.

In less than ten seconds, their attackers were down, either dead or wounded. Sean's decision to shoot first had caught them totally off-guard.

Lights were coming on all over town. Getting back to the river wasn't going to be easy. They ran across half-dressed guards and didn't hesitate to take them out. Men came out of houses with rifles. Sean yelled at one to get back in his house. "Bullets are flying!"

"Yeah, and I hope they all hit you, you son of a bitch." He fired at Sean, missing.

"What are you doing?" screamed Sean.

"Preserving my way of life, you asshole. What do you

think?" He fired again, and this time Sean went down.

"Sean!" screamed Emily.

"I'm fine. Just a scratch." He got up.

"Not this time," yelled the man.

Ben shot him in the chest and the man went flying backwards. Ben looked at Sean and raised his arms, as if to say, "I had no choice."

It wasn't going well. They were ready for the don's army. What they weren't prepared for was the resistance by the residents. Sean had touched on it, but no one had really believed him. It was real.

Another resident came out of the darkness and aimed at Frank. Two rounds from Sean's M-16 took him down. They were getting close to the river.

Two blocks up along the river, they heard more shots. The reinforcements from the hill were engaged in their own battle.

"Frank, you and Lila get everyone across. We'll hold the fort until you're gone, then we're going for Aaron.

"Ben?" Lila looked at him.

"Go. I love you. Go!"

*****

They went. With Frank leading the way, they maneuvered behind old equipment and junk long since forgotten. They almost reached the crossing point and were next to an upside-down boat when they heard a voice yell, "Don't go any further. Put your weapons down. I really don't want to kill women and kids, but by God I will if you don't surrender."

Lila looked in his direction. It was one man in a uniform,

pointing an M-16 at them.

She looked at Frank, who nodded. They both set down their rifles. Lila heard more gunshots from further down the river. Reinforcements were too far away to help.

"Did you really think you were going to get away?" He seemed to be a high-ranking officer. "We have too much at stake here. This town is the future of this country and you people are way too dangerous. As soon as my men get here we'll take you to the don and see what he wants to do with you."

Frank moved to be closer to his family, and the man shot. Frank fell to the ground. Brenda and Sophie screamed and ran to him.

"If anyone else wants to move you can get the. …" He let out an "umph" and fell to the ground, a crossbow bolt sticking out of his chest.

Lila turned around to see Katie with her crossbow propped on the top of the boat. She looked up at Lila, not with fear or tears, but with a look of determination.

"He hurt Sophie's dad."

Lila ran to Frank. He was trying to stand up.

"Not hurt bad," he said, and looked down at his side.

The man was obviously inexperienced with an M-16, and had actually missed with his shot and hit the ground at Frank's feet. But the bullet splintered a piece of sharp rock that embedded itself in Frank's side.

Lila looked back at Katie. The determined look was still on her face. She had no regrets. Would she later?

*****

Once Frank and Lila and the others were around the corner of the power plant, Ben and Sean took off in the direction of the town hall. They made it a block without having to fire their weapons. Then they rounded a corner and were met by three townspeople, all holding weapons.

"Stop right there," commanded one of them.

Ben and Sean each raised their rifles, pointing at the men. It was a standoff.

"Look," said Sean calmly. He could see the others were nervous. "We're not here to hurt you. We were just rescuing some people from the don. That's all."

"That you, Sean? Haven't seen you in years."

"Hey, Mike. We're just going in to get Aaron, then we're gone. Please. Put down your weapons. We really don't want to hurt you."

The men hesitated, looked at each other, then complied.

"Thanks," said Sean. They continued on their way.

They hadn't gone more than a hundred feet further when they were confronted by four heavily-armed men in uniform. They were on three sides of them.

"Drop your weapons or you're dead," said one.

They set their weapons on the ground and lifted their arms in the air. The man closest to Sean raised his pistol, as if to shoot, when his head exploded. A second later, another man's head erupted into a red spray. Two seconds later, all four of them were lying in a massive pool of blood.

A voice called out, "You wuss, Bullock. You were going to surrender?"

It was Aaron!

Chapter 31

Aaron heard the shots. It was time to leave. He didn't know who was shooting, or why, but he figured the don had finally pissed off the wrong people. He wanted to smile in satisfaction, but that would have to wait. Emily was out there and might get caught in the crossfire.

Definitely time to leave.

The funny thing was, he could have left whenever he wanted. He would have told Emily that the day they let her come to visit, but they were right there, listening to every word. So she had to leave upset and scared. Well, they'd pay for that. In particular, the don would pay for that. He didn't leave because he wanted to know what the don had in store for him. Besides, getting out of his "jail cell"—actually a windowless store room in the town hall—would be one thing. Getting out of town with Emily would be another. But the shooting was the sign.

When he'd been brought to the town hall a week earlier, he was taken directly to the don's office. The walls of the office were covered with photos of Chicago from back in the 1930s. Chicago souvenirs covered his desk and bookcases. Aaron thought it was a little over-the-top.

He had never actually had a conversation with Bolli—who always seemed to go out of his way to avoid Aaron—so any opinion he had formed was strictly from his observations of how the town was run. Based on that, his opinions weren't positive.

Bolli stood behind his desk. An unimpressive-looking man, Bolli reminded Aaron of a rodent—small and thin-featured— and he didn't look one bit Italian.

"We finally meet," announced Bolli in a too-loud voice.

"We've met a few times," reminded Aaron. "Just never really talked."

"That's what I meant." He seemed unsettled by Aaron's presence—almost nervous. This was some big-time Chicago mobster?

Bolli continued. "Word is that you don't like it here. That you're planning to leave."

"So?"

"Just curious why."

"Never heard of a town where you got called into the mayor's office if you intended to leave. Seems just a little weird."

"The times are a little weird. The world isn't what it once was."

"No shit."

"The fact is, I need you here. The town needs you here. We need people who can help protect the town."

"From what?"

"Not from what, from who."

"From whom, not from who."

Bolli gave him a look.

"Hey, I live with a teacher. I can't get away with that kind of stuff."

Bolli was pissed. Aaron obviously wasn't afraid of him.

He tried again. "Do you have any idea about the importance of this town?"

"Because we have power?"

"Of course because we have power!"

"So what?" Aaron was enjoying this.

Bolli took a deep breath. "To my knowledge, we are the only town in the whole country with power. That's an amazing accomplishment."

"You say that like you had something to do with it. You showed up when it was already on. The person responsible was a good man named Baxter."

"I'm aware of that and grateful to him for it. But it's my responsibility to take it from here. Paradise is a small town now, but it's growing ..."

"Because you are kidnapping people and bringing them here," interrupted Aaron.

"I admit that sometimes my men get a little over-zealous in their recruiting, and I apologize for that, but you have to admit that once the people are here, they seem to like it."

Aaron couldn't argue with that. People did seem to embrace the electricity quickly once they arrived. It had an intoxicating effect.

"It's up to me to transform Paradise from a town to a city. I can see it in a few years as the center of the country—not just geographically, but politically and emotionally. I want it to be the place where people come to get a sense of what this country was—and can be again. I want Paradise to expand, the electricity going in all directions. I want to tear down the burned-out remains next to us and rebuild. But until then, it's all very fragile and needs to be protected."

"So I ask again, from what, or whom?"

"From those out to destroy it. I want this country to return to what it once was, what we all once had. There are people who want to control that."

"Like you?"

"Like others! I've brought stability to this town. You were here when I arrived. You know how chaotic everything was with the power struggles. Other groups want what we have and will stop at nothing to get it."

"What groups? There aren't enough people out there to form a big enough group to take you over."

"Oh, but there are. And they are almost crazed at the idea of controlling this much power—figuratively and literally."

Crazed would be a good word for it, thought Aaron. "I'll be honest with you, Marco. It's not for me. I don't want to live in a reminder of the past. I want to live in the hope and reality of the future. You're right. The world isn't what it was, and most people have gotten used to that fact. We may have electricity here, but from what I've seen, people aren't enjoying life like they used to. They just seem to be desperately clinging to the little reminder of what they once had. That's not growth, and it's not for me."

"I'm trying to build something here and you're fighting me on it. I can't let you leave, and at this point I can't let you stay.

I've got to figure out what to do with you."

The don obviously hadn't figured that out, because Aaron had gone a week sitting in that empty room without any word from Bolli.

*****

He pounded on the door and called to the guard.

"Sammy, you out there? What's going on?"

"Don't know. Shut up while I check."

Sammy was right outside the door. Being a store room, the door opened outward. Aaron kicked it and it flew open, striking Sammy and momentarily stunning him. It was more time than Aaron needed. He grabbed Sammy's arm and savagely brought it down over his knee, shattering the elbow. Sammy opened his mouth to scream when Aaron struck him in the throat. He slumped to the floor, dead.

Aaron gave a quick thought to finding Bolli, but dismissed it. He needed to find Emily. He grabbed Sammy's M-16 and ran out the door. He traversed the streets. All around him people were running—men in uniforms and townspeople—all with weapons. All hell had broken loose.

He was rounding a corner when he heard raised voices. He was curious. He stopped and quietly moved toward them. When he was about fifty feet away, he suddenly had a clear view. Four heavily-armed men pointing guns at two others. It was Sean!

Holy shit! He thought. The person standing next to Sean was his brother, Ben. It had to be. He was older, but there was no doubt. They had set down their weapons and were raising their hands.

One of the guards raised his handgun as if to shoot. It was Conklin. He'd always been an asshole. Well, now he'd be a dead asshole.

Aaron aimed and fired, all in one motion. Conklin's head exploded.

And then he calmly took three more shots.

Chapter 32

Out from the darkness stepped his brother. Ben could already feel the tears running down his cheeks. All around they could hear yelling. Guns were being fired, probably at nonexistent targets. Somewhere a fire had started. But at that moment, in that spot, none of the chaos existed.

Sean had stepped back to give the brothers their space and to keep watch.

Ben and Aaron approached each other. Not a word was spoken between them. Ben noticed his brother's face was also shiny with tears. They were three feet apart, each taking in the scene. And then they closed the gap and embraced. The years of loss fell away as they shook in each other's arms, alternately crying and laughing. The tears continued to flow. They pulled back and stared at each other.

"Hey," said Aaron.

"Hey."

And then they embraced again, still barely believing the reality of the situation.

"Gotta go," said Sean urgently at the sound of an approaching group.

"Where's Emily?" asked Aaron.

"She's safe," answered Ben. "Where's the don? I have a score to settle."

"Probably in the town hall," said Aaron. "But he's mine."

"Already bossing me around," said Ben, as they started for the showdown with the don.

Out of the corner of his eye, Ben spied some round objects attached to the belts of the dead men. Hand grenades. He grabbed four of them and followed Aaron and Sean.

All around them confusion reigned. Nearer the river a battle was raging between the Yellowstone crew and Bolli's armed force. But there was more, and it confused Ben.

They stopped for momentary cover.

Ben heard more shouting. He heard Aaron's name mentioned, followed with the word "bastard."

"I don't get it," he said suddenly.

"Get what?" asked Aaron as they started back on their way.

"The anger of the townspeople. I had to kill one who shot Sean."

Aaron looked at Sean.

"I'm fine," his friend answered.

"What I'm saying," continued Ben, "is that I can understand people wanting to protect their town, but this is different. It's like they've gone wild. There's almost a hatred coming from some of them."

"It's fear," said Aaron. "Not the fear of being attacked, but the fear of losing it all."

"The electricity?"

"Yeah, but more what it represents. It's their one remaining connection to their old life."

"But look what it's doing to them," said Ben.

And then it hit him.

It all became clear to me in that moment. For over a year I had heard about the great "evil," and had seen the effects of it all along our trip west. All of the violence and negativity had brought us to Paradise and to the don, leading me to assume that the don was the great evil. But it wasn't the don after all. It was the electricity itself. More specifically, the real evil was people's obsession with the electricity.

In our old world, electricity was a simple necessity. It wasn't thought of as being positive or negative. It was what it was. We couldn't live without it, but we didn't need to. It was always there. We learned to appreciate its importance during blackouts—the only time we gave it more than a second thought.

But now it had become an unhealthy need—one that people were willing to kill for. It was obvious to me that the power would never extend much beyond the perimeter of Paradise. And yet, the fight to control it would go on indefinitely. From the day Baxter turned the electricity on, the leadership of Paradise became a revolving door—at least until the don showed up. When he was gone—which would be very soon if Aaron had his way—the door would start to revolve once again.

It was a disease. In this vast country were a few people and communities trying their best to create something positive, and right in the middle of it was this unstoppable mass. Like cancerous cells, it was just going to keep spreading, eventually beyond the borders of Paradise, to infect the healthy communities like Monett and Yellowstone.

I knew what I had to do.

They had reached the entrance to the town hall. Twenty-five feet away, a single guard manned the door.

Sean pulled out a large knife.

"The battles are a few blocks away. I'd rather not advertise our presence by shooting him."

Ben put his hand on Sean's shoulder.

"Let me."

He took the crossbow off his back, loaded it, and aimed. The man was looking out at a small fire that had started a few streets over.

Ben pulled the trigger and the man sank to the ground, a shaft protruding from his head.

Aaron looked at him with pride. "Impressive. Let's go."

Dealing with Marco Bolli turned out to be simple, and more than a little pathetic. They found him hiding under his desk in the opulent office he had created for himself. He pleaded for his life and tried to explain that he wasn't really Bolli at all.

Ben had seen enough killing and was almost ready to walk away, but Aaron wasn't so charitable. They left Bolli dead, crumpled in a heap under his desk—an appropriately ignoble ending to his attempted legacy.

They left the building and were going to work their way back to the river.

But Ben wasn't done.

The gunfire from upriver had pretty much ceased—Ben hoped it meant that the Yellowstone crew had pulled back—but the town was still alive with shouting. He heard Aaron and Sean's names spewed a few times, and the occasional rifle sounded.

"This is insane," said Sean.

"It's got to stop," answered Ben. They were passing the parking area for all of the trucks.

"Can I have two of those grenades?" Aaron asked Ben.

"Yeah, but only two. I have plans for the other two."

They looked at him, understanding showing in their faces.

"I'll meet you at the river in fifteen," said Ben.

"Okay. Good luck," said Aaron.

Ben took off. He wound his way behind some buildings, and in just a couple of minutes found himself in front of the power plant. No one was around. The noise of the search parties had now moved to the town hall. He found the main door. It was locked with a makeshift padlock and bracket. Ben searched around and found a piece of metal that he used to break the bracket. The door swung open.

Ben found a light switch, flicked it on, and closed the door behind him. He was in a spacious room with offices on the left and a wire fence on the right. Behind the fence were panels upon panels of circuit boards and wires—the black heart of the town. He didn't need to worry about the power generating equipment—probably downstairs closer to the river—this would be enough.

Again, a padlock was all that stood between him and his goal. He quickly disposed of it, then looked around and spied a storage room over near the offices. He entered it and found what he was looking for—paint thinner.

He carried the can over to the panel room and splashed the liquid around, over and under the panels. From outside he heard a muffled explosion, then a moment later a second one. These were followed a few seconds after by a series of much larger explosions—the tanker trucks.

Ben placed his two hand grenades in what he imagined would be effective spots. Before pulling the pins, he went back to the door leading outside and checked to make sure it wasn't blocked or wedged closed in any way.

Satisfied, he went back to the panels. He was shaking from what he was about to do. He had a moment's doubt, but only a moment. He breathed in to calm himself, but the air was strong with the odor of paint thinner and he coughed.

It was time.

He pulled the pin from the first grenade, then quickly pulled the second and hightailed it out of there. He was halfway out the door when the first one went off. He was surprised at the lack of intensity of the explosion. He had expected more. Just a product of the movie generation, he supposed, where all the special effects were exaggerated. A moment later the second one went off. Although weaker than he thought, they had done their job. All of the lights in the town went dark at once.

The shouting was getting closer. He made his way around the side of the building toward the river.

And then he heard it. A "whump" sounded from inside the building and flames were showing through some small upper windows.

His job was complete.

*****

Ben caught up with Aaron and Sean at the edge of the river and they made their way across. They weren't pursued or fired upon. The townspeople had too much on their plates to worry about at this point.

They made it to the top of the bluff a half hour later, where they were greeted by Lila, Katie, Emily, and the others. The Yellowstone group had been fortunate. Other than a few minor wounds, everyone had made it through the battle unscathed.

Ben introduced Lila and Katie to Aaron, and then they all looked down on Paradise, relieved that it was over.

Ben looked at Aaron. "I have a bone to pick with you."

Aaron raised his eyebrows.

"Sean says you were in my room at the house. I told you never to go in my room without my permission."

"Get over it, little brother."

Epilogue

I watched it burn for hours, until there was nothing left but the smoldering hulks of trucks and what was left of the brick walls of the power plant. It was now dawn and Lila was safely on her way home with Katie, along with the others. A few had stayed behind for a while, but eventually headed back. I was alone. I told them I'd catch up. They understood. I needed the time to let the magnitude of what I'd done sink in.

Was it the right thing? The decision to blow the power plant was solely mine. We could have accomplished the mission without destroying the plant. I could have walked away. But deep down I knew that wasn't an option. It had been the source of so much misery and so much pain for so many. But in my zeal to destroy it and all it stood for, had I affected our future? Was it just hubris on my part? Right here were the tools necessary to bring our society back to a semblance of what it once was. Had I just set the future of the country back, or had I somehow contributed to its healing? Over time we could have had power again — all of us maybe. But even the word "power" was now distasteful to me — even when meant in the simplest terms of "electrical" power. It seemed the one power bred the other, and I had had enough of that.

No, I had just played God—for right or wrong—and I was going to have to live with the consequences. As much as I was admired by some for all that Lila and I had done in the early days, I was now going to be hated by others. So be it. I made my choice and I was willing to live with it.

What would happen to Paradise now? Would it survive? I didn't have any answers to that. I hoped it would. I hoped the people there could adapt and become stronger.

Lila told me of Katie killing the man. I never wanted that for her. I wanted her to live a peaceful life. I wanted all the violence in our life to be in the past. Well, maybe it finally was. We would talk to Katie about the incident, but somehow, oddly enough, I wasn't too concerned. Katie didn't see the man as anything different from a marauding animal that had to be killed. Nothing more. It was just how she saw life. It seemed healthy to me.

Those of us who made up this new world in Yellowstone were the strong ones. We had all survived the initial event simply by luck, but it wasn't luck that had brought us together. It was strength and it was the will to live. We earned our place in Yellowstone, and we were happy with the simple life. Everything we did now was conscious. We were living fully. For Lila and me, it was the best of both worlds: the simple life we had enjoyed in the Smokies, along with the community that was so important for Katie's future. We had good friends. We even had family now. It was time to settle down into the life we had earned.

No, I did the right thing in Paradise. Somewhere, someone else will master the old technology and will make it available. Over time— maybe twenty years, maybe a hundred—it will begin to show up *again in society. Maybe by then we will be ready to embrace it again. And maybe this time we will do it right.*

The End

ABOUT THE AUTHOR

Andrew Cunningham is the author of fifteen novels, including the *"Lies" Mystery Series*: **All Lies, Fatal Lies, Vegas Lies, Secrets & Lies, Blood Lies**, and **Buried Lies;** the post-apocalyptic *Eden Rising Series*: **Eden Rising, Eden Lost, Eden's Legacy,** and **Eden's Survival**; the *Yestertime Time Travel Series:* **Yestertime, The Yestertime Effect,** and **The Yestertime Warning;** the disaster/terrorist thriller **Deadly Shore,** and the award-winning thriller **Wisdom Spring.** As A.R. Cunningham, he has written a series of five children's mysteries in the *Arthur MacArthur* series. Born in England, Andrew was a long-time resident of Cape Cod. He and his wife now live in Florida. Please visit his website at *arcnovels.com*, or his Facebook page, *Author Andrew Cunningham.*

Made in United States
Orlando, FL
31 May 2023

33673341R00153